A mysterious voice from the telephone; a beautiful Chinese girl shot dead; a rich old man with a troubled conscience; a private investigator involved in murder; a Chinese prostitute who talked too much; and a coffin. These are some of the intriguing ingredients of James Hadley Chase's splendid thriller. It is definitely a book to keep you awake long after your bedtime.

Also by James Hadley Chase in
Panther Books

James Hadley Chase

A Coffin From Hong Kong

Panther

Granada Publishing Limited
Published in 1964 by Panther Books Ltd
Frogmore, St Albans, Herts AL2 2NF
Reprinted 1964, 1966, 1968, 1969, 1973, 1976

First published in Great Britain by
Robert Hale Ltd 1962
Copyright © James Hadley Chase 1962
Made and printed in Great Britain by
C. Nicholls & Company Ltd
The Philips Park Press, Manchester
Set in Intertype Plantin

CHAPTER ONE

1

I was just about to shut down the office for the night when the telephone bell rang. The time was ten minutes past six o'clock. It had been a dull, long and unprofitable day: no visitors, a mail I had dropped into the trash basket without even slitting an envelope, and now this first telephone call.

I lifted the receiver and said, "Nelson Ryan." My voice as alert and eager as I could make it.

There was a pause. Over the open line I could hear the sound of an aircraft engine start up. The din beat against my ear for a brief moment, then faded to background noise as if the caller had closed the door of the telephone booth.

"Mr. Ryan?"

A man's voice: deep toned and curt.

"That's right."

"You are a private investigator?"

"Right again."

There was another pause. I listened to his slow, heavy breathing: he was probably listening to mine. Then he said: "I have only a few minutes. I'm at the airport. I want to hire you."

I reached for a scratch pad.

"What's your name and your address?" I asked.

"John Hardwick, 33 Connaught Boulevard."

As I scribbled the address on the pad, I asked, "What is it you want me to do, Mr. Hardwick?"

"I want you to watch my wife." There was another pause as another aircraft took off. He said something that was blotted out by the high whine of the jet's engines.

"I didn't get that, Mr. Hardwick."

He waited until the jet had become airborne, then speaking rapidly, he said, "My business takes me regularly twice a month to New York. I have the idea that while I'm away, my wife isn't behaving herself. I want you to watch her. I'll be back the day after tomorrow—Friday. I want to know what she does while I'm away. What will it cost?"

This wasn't the kind of business I welcomed, but at least it was better than nothing.

"Just what is your business, Mr. Hardwick?"

He spoke with a touch of impatience. "I'm with Herron, the plastic people."

Herron Corporation was one of the biggest concerns on this strip of the Pacific Coast. A quarter of Pasadena City's prosperity came from them.

"Fifty dollars a day and expenses," I said, jacking up my usual fee by ten bucks.

"That's all right. I'll send you three hundred dollars right away as a retainer. I want you to follow my wife wherever she goes. If she doesn't leave home, I want to know if anyone visits her. Will you do this?"

For three hundred dollars I would have done much harder things. I said, "I'll do it, but couldn't you come in and see me, Mr. Hardwick? I like to meet my clients."

"I understand that but I have only just decided to take action. I'm on my way to New York, but I'll see you on Friday. I just want to be sure you will watch her while I'm away."

"You can be sure of that," I said, then paused to let another jet whine down the runway. "I'll need a description of your wife, Mr. Hardwick."

"Thirty-three Connaught Boulevard," he said. "They are calling me. I must go. I'll see you on Friday," and the line went dead.

I replaced the receiver and took a cigarette from the box on the desk. I lit the cigarette with the desk lighter and blew smoke towards the opposite wall.

I had been working as an investigator for the past five years, and during that time, I had run into a number of screwballs. This John Hardwick could be just another screwball, but somehow I didn't think he was. He sounded like a man under pressure. Maybe he had been worrying for months about the way his wife had been behaving. Maybe for a long time he had suspected her of getting up to tricks when he was away and suddenly, as he was leaving for another business trip, he had finally decided to check on her. It was the kind of thing a worried, unhappy man might do—a split-second impulse. All the same, I didn't like it much. I don't like anonymous clients. I don't like disembodied voices on the telephone. I like to know with whom I am dealing. This set-up seemed a shade too hurried and a shade too contrived.

While I was turning over the information I had got from him, I heard footfalls coming along the passage. A tap sounded on the frosted panel of my door, then the door opened.

An Express messenger dropped a fat envelope on my desk and offered me his book for my signature.

He was a little guy with freckles, young and still clinging to an enthusiasm for life that had begun to slip away from me. As I signed his book, his eyes sneered around the small shabby room, taking in the damp stain on the ceiling, the dust on the bookcase,

6

the unimpressive desk, the worn clients' chair and the breast and bottom calendar on the wall.

When he had gone I opened the envelope. It contained thirty ten-dollar bills. Typed on a plain card were the words:

From John Hardwick, 33 Connaught Boulevard, Pasadena City.

For a moment I was puzzled how he could have got the money to me so quickly, then I decided he must have a credit rating with the Express Messenger Company and had telephoned them immediately after telephoning me. Their offices were just across the street from my office block.

I pulled the telephone book towards me and turned up the Hardwicks. There was no John Hardwick. I eased myself out of my desk chair and plodded across the room to consult the Street Directory. It told me Jack S. Myers, Jnr., and not John Hardwick, lived at 33 Connaught Boulevard.

I stroked my six o'clock shadow while I considered the situation. I remembered that Connaught Boulevard was an out-of-the-way road up on Palma Mountain, about three miles from the centre of the city. It was the kind of district where people might rent their homes while they were on vacation: this could be the situation as regards John Hardwick and his wife. He might possibly be an executive of Herron Corporation, waiting for his own house to be built, and in the meantime, he had rented 33 Connaught Boulevard from Jack S. Myers, Jnr.

I had only once been to Connaught Boulevard and that was some time ago. The property there had been run up just after the war: nothing very special. Most of the places were bungalows, half brick, half timber. The best thing about Connaught Boulevard was its view of the city and the sea, and if you wanted it, its seclusion.

The more I thought about this assignment, the less I liked it. I hadn't even a description of the woman I had been hired to watch. If I hadn't been paid the three hundred dollars I wouldn't have touched the job without first seeing Hardwick, but as I had been paid, I felt I had to do what he wanted me to do.

I locked up my office, then crossing the outer office, I locked the outer door and started for the elevator.

My next-door neighbour, an Industrial Chemist, was still toiling for a living. I could hear his clear, baritone voice dictating either to a recorder or to his secretary.

I took the elevator to the ground floor and crossing the street, I went into the Quick Snack Bar where I usually ate. I asked Sparrow, the counter man, to cut me a couple of ham and chicken sandwiches.

Sparrow, a tall thin bird with a shock of white hair, took an interest in my affairs. He wasn't a bad guy, and from time to

7

time, I would cheer him up with a flock of lies about adventures he liked to imagine happened to me.

"Are you on a job tonight, Mr. Ryan?" he asked eagerly as he began to make the sandwiches.

"That's right," I said. "I'm spending the night with a client's wife, seeing she doesn't get into mischief."

His mouth dropped open as he goggled at me.

"Is that a fact? What's she like, Mr. Ryan?"

"You know Liz Taylor?"

He nodded, leaning forward and breathing heavily.

"You know Marilyn Monroe?"

His Adam's apple jumped convulsively.

"I sure do."

I gave him a sad smile.

"She's like neither of them."

He blinked, then realising I was kidding him, he grinned.

"Poking my nose where it shouldn't be poked, huh?" he said. "I guess I asked for that one."

"Hurry it up, Sparrow," I said. "I have my living to earn."

He put the sandwiches in a paper sack.

"Don't do anything you're not paid to do, Mr. Ryan," he said, giving me the sack.

The time was now twenty minutes to seven. I got in my car and drove out to Connaught Boulevard. I didn't hurry. By the time I was driving up the mountain road, the late September sun was sinking behind the peak of the mountain.

The bungalows in Connaught Boulevard were screened from the road by box hedges or flowering shrubs. I drove slowly past No. 33. Big double gates hid the property. Some twenty yards or so further up the road was a lay-by which commanded a splendid view of the sea. I pulled in there, cut the engine and shifted from the driver's seat to the passenger's seat. From this position I had a clear view of the double gates.

There wasn't anything for me to do but wait. This was something I was reasonably good at. If you're crazy enough to pick on a career such as mine, patience is the main necessary ingredient.

During the next hour, three or four cars drove past. The drivers, men returning from the toils of earning a living, glanced at me as they went by. I hoped I looked like a man waiting for a girl friend, and not like a dick watching a client's wife.

A girl, wearing skin tight slacks and a sweater, walked past my parked car. A poodle trotted along just ahead of her, visiting the trees enthusiastically. The girl glanced at me while I let my eyes browse over her shape. She found I was a lot less interesting than I found her. I watched regretfully as she disappeared into the gloom.

By nine o'clock it was dark. I took out the paper sack and ate the sandwiches. I gave myself a slug of whisky from the bottle I kept in the glove compartment.

It had been a long, dull wait. The double gates of No. 33 had been as active as a stuffed pike. But now it was dark enough for me to take the initiative. I left the car and crossed the road. I opened one of the double gates and looked into a small neat garden. There was just light enough to make out a lawn, flowers and a path that led to a compact bungalow with what looked like a veranda.

The bungalow was in darkness. I came to the conclusion that there was no one at home. To make sure, I walked around the back, but no lights showed there either.

I returned to my car, feeling depressed. It appeared that as soon as her husband had left for the airport, Mrs. Hardwick had left home.

There was nothing I could do now but to sit there in the hope she would return sometime during the night. With three hundred dollars still nagging at my conscience, I settled down to wait.

Sometime around three o'clock in the morning, I fell asleep.

The first rays of the sun, striking through the windshield of the car brought me sharply awake. I had a crick in my neck, a nagging ache in my spine and a guilty feeling when I realised I had slept for three hours when I should have been earning my three hundred dollars.

Coming up the road was a milk delivery truck. I watched the milkman stop and start as he delivered milk to each bungalow. He drove past No. 33, then stopped just opposite me to deliver milk to No. 35.

As he came out, I joined him. He was an elderly man whose face showed much background of hard living and toil. He looked inquiringly at me, pausing with his milk bottles in their wire basket clutched in his hand.

"You forgot No. 33," I said. "Everyone's got milk but No. 33."

He looked me over, his old eyes curious.

"They happen to be away," he said. "What's it to you, mister?"

I could see he was the kind you don't take liberties with. I had no wish to have a cop on my neck so I took out my professional card and handed it to him. He examined it carefully, then whistling gently through his teeth, he returned the card to me.

"You don't call on No. 33?" I asked.

"Sure I do, but they're away for a month."

"Who are they?"

He considered the question for a moment.

"Mr. and Mrs. Myers."

"I understand Mr. and Mrs. Hardwick live there now."

He put down the wire basket and shifted his hat to the back of his head.

"Right now no one lives there, mister," he said, scratching his forehead. "I would know if there was anyone there. People have to have milk and I'm the one who delivers it up here. I don't deliver milk to No. 33 because no one lives there this month."

"I see," I said, but I didn't. "You don't think Mr. Myers rented his place to this other guy?"

"I've served Mr. Myers for eight years," he told me. "He's never hired out his place to anyone. He always goes away this month for a month." He picked up his wire basket. I could see he was bored with me now and wanted to get on with his good work.

"You don't know of any John Hardwick in this district?" I asked without much hope.

"Not up here," he said. "I'd know. I know everyone up here," and nodding his head, he went off to his truck and drove up the road to No. 37.

My first reaction was to wonder if I had got the address right, but I knew I had. Hardwick had written it down, besides telling me.

Then why should he have paid me three hundred dollars to sit outside an empty bungalow? Maybe the milkman was wrong, but I didn't think he was.

I walked back to No. 33 and pushed open one of the double gates. In the light of the early morning sun, I didn't have to go up the path to prove to myself the bungalow was empty. Wooden shutters concealed the windows; something I hadn't seen in the darkness. The bungalow had a deserted, shut down appearance.

I had a sudden creepy feeling. Could this mysterious John Hardwick, for reasons best known to himself, have wanted me out of the way and had sent me on this wild goose chase just for that reason? I couldn't believe anyone in his right mind would have squandered three hundred dollars to get rid of me for twelve hours. I felt I couldn't be that important, but the idea nagged. I suddenly wanted to get to my office more urgently than I wanted a shave, a shower and coffee strong enough to lean on.

I hurried back to my car and drove fast down the mountain road. At this hour of the morning there was no traffic and I reached my office block as the street clock struck seven. Leaving the car, I entered the lobby where the janitor was leaning against a broom, breathing heavily and sneering to himself. He gave me a dull, stony look and then turned away. He was a man who hated everyone, including himself.

I rode up to the fourth floor and walked fast down the corridor to the familiar door bearing the legend in flaking black letters: *Nelson Ryan. Investigator.*

I took out my keys, but on second thoughts, reached for the door handle and turned it. The door wasn't locked although I had locked it when I had left the previous evening. I pushed open the

10

door and looked into the small outer office that contained a table on which lay some dog eared magazines, four well worn leather lounging chairs and a strip of carpet: a gesture to anyone with tender feet.

The inner door, leading to my office stood ajar. This too had been locked before I had left.

Again aware of the creepy feeling, I crossed to the door and pushed it wide open.

Sitting, facing me in the clients' chair was a lovely-looking Chinese girl, her hands folded rather primly in her lap. She was wearing a green and silver Cheongsam, slit up either side to show off her beautiful legs. She looked peaceful and not even surprised. From the small bloodstain over her left breast, I guessed she had been shot quickly and expertly: so quickly, she had had no chance even to be scared. Whoever had shot her had done a good, swift job.

Moving as if I were wading through water, I entered the room and touched the side of her cold face. She had been dead some hours.

Taking in a long deep breath, I reached for the telephone and called the police.

2

While waiting for the cops to arrive, I took a closer look at my dead Asian visitor. At a guess she had been around twenty-three or four and apparently not short of money. I assumed this since her clothes seemed expensive, her stockings sheer nylon and her shoes nearly brand new. Also she was well groomed: her nails were immaculate and her hair impeccable. I had no means of knowing who she was. She had no handbag. I assumed the killer had taken it. I couldn't imagine a woman as well turned out as this one would go around without a handbag.

Having satisfied myself that she was anonymous, I went into the other room and waited for the sound of trampling feet that would tell me the boys were arriving. I didn't have to wait long. Within ten minutes of my telephone call they came swarming over me like ants over a lump of sugar.

The last to arrive was Detective Lieutenant Dan Retnick. I had known him off and on for the past four years. He was an under-sized bird with thin, foxy features and a snappy line in clothes. The only reason why he held his position on the city's police force was because he had been lucky enough to have married the Mayor's sister. As a police officer he was about as useful as a hole in a bucket. Luckily for him there had been no major crime in Pasadena City since he had got his appointment. This affair would be the first murder case since he had been upped to Detective Lieutenant from a desk sergeant in a small, unimportant cop house along the Coast.

But I'll say this for him: even though he hadn't the brains to solve a child's crossword puzzle, he certainly looked the part of an efficient tough cop as he breezed into my office with Sergeant Pulski, his side kick, trampling along in his rear.

Sergeant Pulski was a big man with a red fleshy face, small vicious eyes and two fists that seemed to be itching all the time to connect with a human jaw. He had less brains than Retnick if that is possible, but what he lacked in mental equipment, he made up in muscle.

Neither of them looked at me as they came in. They went into my office and stared for a long time at the dead woman, then while Pulski was going through the motions of being a police officer, Retnick joined me in the outer room.

He now looked a little worried and a lot less breezy.

"Okay, shamus, give with the story," he said, sitting on the desk and swinging his immaculately polished shoes. "She a client of yours?"

"I don't know who she is or what she's doing here," I said. "I found her like that when I opened up this morning."

He chewed on his dead cigar while he stared his hard cop stare. "You usually open up this early?"

I gave him the story without holding anything back. He listened. Pulski who had finished acting the police officer with the boys in my office, propped up the door-post and listened too.

"As soon as I found out the bungalow was empty, I came straight back here," I concluded. "I figured something was going on, but I didn't expect this."

"Where's her handbag?" Retnick said.

"I don't know. While I was waiting for you to arrive I searched for it, but couldn't find it. She must have had one. Maybe the killer took it away with him."

He scratched the side of his jaw, took the dead cigar out of his mouth and looked at it, then put it back into his face again.

"What did she have in it, shamus, that tempted you to kill her?" he demanded finally.

There was never anything subtle about Retnick. I knew when I telephoned for the police, I would be his suspect number one.

"Even if she had had the Koh-i-Noor diamond, I wouldn't have been that dumb to knock her off here," I said patiently. "I would have tailed her back to where she lived and fixed her there."

"How do you explain what she was doing here and how she got in if you had locked up?"

"I could make a guess."

His eyes narrowed and he cocked his head on one side.

"Go ahead and guess."

"I think this woman had business with me. A guy calling himself John Hardwick didn't want her to talk to me. I don't know why nor do I know what she wanted to talk to me about—I'm just guessing. It's my guess Hardwick sent me to sit outside an empty bungalow to be sure I wouldn't be in my office when she arrived. I think he was waiting here for her. My locks are nothing special. He wouldn't have any trouble opening the doors. He was probably sitting at my desk when she walked in. The fact she doesn't look scared makes me think she didn't know this guy and thought he was me. After she had said her say, he shot her. It was a quick expert shot. She didn't have time even to change the expression on her face."

Retnick looked at Pulski.

"If we don't watch out, this shamus will be stealing our jobs."

Pulski removed something from a back tooth and spat it on my carpet. He didn't say anything: it wasn't his job to talk. He was a professional listener.

Retnick thought for a moment. It was a process that apparently gave him some pain. Finally, he said, "I'll tell you what makes your guess stink, bright boy. This guy called you from the airport which is two miles from here. If you're not lying, you left your office just after six. He couldn't have got here much before seven-thirty the way the traffic is on that highway at that time, and anyone, even a yellow skin, would know that's after business hours. She wouldn't have come here on the off-chance of finding you here. She would have telephoned first."

"What makes you so sure she didn't? Maybe she did and Hardwick was in my office to take the call. Maybe he told her he would be waiting for her and for her to come right along."

By his change of expression I knew he was irritated with himself for not having worked this out for himself.

The M.O., plus two interns, plus the usual stretcher appeared in the doorway.

Pulski reluctantly pushed himself off the door-post and took the M.O., a fussy little guy with a lemon sour face, into the inner room to view the remains.

Retnick adjusted a pearl stickpin in his tie.

"She shouldn't be difficult to trace," he said as if he were talking to himself. "When a yellow skin is as pretty as this one, she gets noticed. When did you say this guy Hardwick was going to call on you?"

"Tomorrow—Friday."

"Think he will?"

"Not a chance."

He nodded his head.

"Yeah." He looked at his watch, then yawned. "You look like hell. Suppose you go get yourself a cup of coffee? Don't go far and don't flap your mouth. I'll be ready to talk to you in about half an hour."

I wasn't kidded for a moment. He wasn't being considerate: he wanted me out of the way.

"I guess I can use some coffee," I said. "Okay for me to go home and take a shower?"

"Who cares how bad you smell?" he said. "Just coffee and where you can be seen."

I took the elevator to the ground floor. Although it was only twenty minutes to eight o'clock, a small crowd had collected to stare at the waiting ambulance and the four police cars parked in front of the building. As I walked to the Quick Snack Bar I heard heavy footfalls behind me. I didn't bother to look around. I expected to drink my coffee under police supervision.

I entered the bar and eased myself up onto a stool. Sparrow, his eyes bugging, tore himself from the window where he was watching the ambulance and looked expectantly at me.

"What's cooking, Mr. Ryan?" he asked, his breath hissing between his teeth.

"A coffee, strong and black and fast," I said, "then two fried eggs on ham."

The big plain-clothes man who had followed me didn't come into the bar. He stood just outside where he could watch me.

Containing his patience with an effort that brought dark circles to his armpits, Sparrow drew coffee and then got busy with the eggs and ham.

"Someone dead, Mr. Ryan?" he asked as he broke the eggs onto the hot-plate.

"What time do you shut down for the night?" I asked, watching the cop outside who scowled at me through the plate-glass window.

"Ten o'clock sharp," Sparrow said, doing an unconscious little jig with impatience. "What's going on across the way?"

"A Chinese woman got herself murdered." I drank some of the coffee. It was hot and strong and good. "I found her in my office half an hour ago."

His Adam's apple did a rock 'n' roll.

"No kidding, Mr. Ryan?"

"Gospel truth." I finished the coffee and pushed the cup towards him. "And again."

"A Chinese woman?"

"Yeah. Don't ask questions. I know as much as you do about it. Did you see a Chinese woman go in my office block after I had left?"

He shook his head as he refilled my cup.

"No. I think I'd have seen her if she had gone in before I shut up. I hadn't much to do last night."

I began to sweat gently. I had an alibi up to half past eight: the time the girl and the poodle had passed me. I had reckoned the Chinese woman had been in my office at that time. After half

14

past eight, I had only me to say I had been sitting all night outside Jack S. Myers Jnr.'s empty bungalow.

"Did you notice any stranger going in there from the time I left to the time you closed?"

"Can't say I did. Around nine the janitor locked up as usual." He served the ham and eggs. "Who killed her?"

"I don't know." I had suddenly lost my appetite. The set-up now began to look bad for me. I knew Retnick. He was essentially a guy who clutched at straws. If I hadn't a cast-iron alibi that would convince an idiot child, he would pounce on me. "You could have missed seeing her, couldn't you?"

"I guess that's right. I wasn't looking out of the window all the time."

Two men came in and ordered breakfast. They asked Sparrow what was going on. After a glance at me, he said he didn't know. One of the men, a fat fellow wearing a Brando leather jacket said, "Someone's got knocked off. That's the blood-wagon outside."

I pushed aside my plate. I just couldn't eat food right now. I finished the coffee and slid off the stool.

Sparrow looked unhappily at me.

"Something wrong, Mr. Ryan?"

"Just too ambitious I guess," I said. "Put it on the slate," and I went out onto the street.

The big cop closed in on me.

"Where do you imagine you're going?" he demanded.

"Back to my office," I told him. "That worry you?"

"When the Lieutenant's ready for you, I'll tell you. Go sit in one of them cars."

I went to one of the police cars and sat in the back. The forty-odd people standing staring, stared at me instead of the ambulance. I lit a cigarette and tried to ignore them.

I sat there smoking and letting my mind work on the past and the present without allowing it to move into the future. The more I considered my position the less I liked it. I had a feeling of being in a trap.

After nearly an hour the two interns came out carrying the stretcher. The Chinese woman, under the sheet, looked small and child-like. The crowd made the usual noise a crowd makes when it is being morbid. The interns loaded the stretcher into the ambulance and drove away. A few minutes later the M.O. came out, and getting in his car, drove after the ambulance.

There was another long wait, then the Homicide boys came out. One of them signalled to the big cop who was standing watching me. They all crammed into their cars and drove away.

The big cop opened the car door and jerked his thumb at me.

"Get moving," he said. "The Lieutenant wants you."

As I started across the sidewalk, Jay Wayde, the Industrial

Chemist, who had the office next to mine came from his car. He joined me in the elevator.

He was three or four years younger than myself: a big, athletic college type with a crew-cut, a sun-tanned complexion and alert eyes. Every now and then we would meet as we left our offices and would ride down in the elevator together to our cars. He seemed a pretty regular fellow and like Sparrow, he had shown an interest in my way of life. I guess most respectable people can't resist the so-called glamour of an investigator's life. He often asked me what excitement I had had, and in the short time we were in the elevator and walking to our cars, I fed him the kind of lies I fed Sparrow.

"What goes on?" he asked as the elevator began its slow climb to the fourth floor.

"I found a dead Chinese woman in my office this morning," I said. "The cops are getting excited about it."

He stared at me.

"Dead?"

"Someone shot her."

This piece of information appeared to stand him on his ear.

"You mean she's been murdered?"

"That's the technical term for it."

"Well! For the love of Mike!"

"I've been saying exactly that since I found her."

"Who killed her?"

"Ah! Now that is the question. What time did you leave your office last night? You hadn't gone when I left."

"Around nine. The janitor was closing up."

"You didn't hear a shot?"

"For God's sake . . . no!"

"When you left did you notice if there was a light on in my office?"

"There wasn't. Didn't I hear you leave about six?"

"That's right."

I was getting rattled now. This Chinese girl must have been murdered after nine o'clock. My alibi was looking sicker than a wet hen.

The elevator came to rest at the fourth floor. We got out. Coming from my office was the janitor and Sergeant Pulski. The janitor looked at me as if I were a two-headed monster. They got into the elevator and sank out of sight.

"Well, I guess you're going to be busy," Wayde said, eyeing the cop standing at my office door. "If there's anything I can do . . ."

"Thanks," I said. "I'll let you know."

Leaving him, I walked past the cop and into the outer office. Apart from match ends on the floor and cigarette butts anywhere but in the ash-trays, the room had a lonely empty look. I went into my office.

16

Lieutenant Retnick was sitting behind my desk. He regarded me with the usual cop stare as I came in, and then waved me to the clients' chair.

There was a smear of dry blood on the back of the chair. I didn't fancy to contact with that so I sat on the arm of the chair.

"You got a gun permit?" he asked.

"Yes."

"What's your gun?"

"A .38 police special."

He laid his hand, palm up, on the blotter.

"Give."

"It's in the top right-hand drawer."

He stared for a long moment, then withdrew his hand.

"It isn't. I've looked through your desk."

I resisted the temptation to wipe away the trickle of cold sweat that began to run down the back of my neck.

"That's where it should be."

He took a cigar from a pigskin case, stripped off the wrapping, pierced the cigar with a match end, then fed the cigar into his face. All the time his small hard eyes locked with mine.

"She was shot with a .38," he said. "The M.O. says she died around three o'clock this morning. Look, Ryan, why don't you come clean? Just what did this yellow skin have in her handbag?"

Keeping my voice calm with an effort, I said, "I may seem to you to be a dumb, stupid peeper, but you can't really believe I would be that dumb and that stupid to knock off a client in my own office with my own gun even if she had all the gold in Fort Knox in her goddam handbag."

He lit the cigar and blew a stream of rank smoke at me.

"I don't know: you might. You might be trying to play it smart, kidding yourself you had dreamed up a water-tight alibi," he said, but there wasn't much conviction in his voice.

"If I had killed her," I went on, "I would have known the time she had died. I wouldn't have given you an alibi for eight-thirty, I would have cooked one up for three o'clock."

He shifted around in my chair while what he used as a brain creaked under pressure.

"What was she doing in your office at that hour in the morning?"

"Want me to guess?"

"Look, Ryan, we haven't had a murder in this city for five years. I've got to have some story to give the Press. Any ideas you've got, I'll listen to. You help us, I'll help you. I could arrest you and toss you in the tank on the evidence I've got against you, but I'm giving you a chance to prove I'm wrong. Go ahead and guess."

"Suppose she was from 'Frisco and not here? Suppose she had to talk urgently with me? Don't ask me why or why she couldn't

17

talk to a private dick in 'Frisco: just suppose this happened. Suppose she decided to take a plane and come here so she could talk to me and suppose she made up her mind about seven last night. She would know she couldn't get here before I had left so she telephoned. Hardwick, having got rid of me, was waiting here to take the call. She told him she was flying here and would be here around three o'clock. He said it was okay and he would be here when she did arrive. When she arrived at the airport, she took a taxi and came here. Hardwick listened to what she had to say, then shot her."

"Using your gun?"

"Using my gun."

"The entrance to this building is locked at nine. The lock hasn't been tampered with. How did Hardwick and the yellow skin get in here?"

"Hardwick must have arrived as soon as I had left and before the janitor locked up. He knew I was out of the way so he could sit right here and wait for the telephone call. When the time came for her to arrive, he went down and let her in. It's a Yale lock. There's no trouble opening it from the inside."

"You ought to write movie scripts," he said sourly. "Is this the yarn you're going to tell the jury?"

"It's worth checking. She would be easily spotted at the airport. The taxi-drivers out there would remember her."

"Supposed it happened the way you say but instead of this unknown Hardwick, you were the one who told her you would wait for her?"

"He's not unknown. If you'll check with the Express Messenger Service you'll find he sent me three hundred dollars. You can check I was outside 33 Connaught Boulevard from seven-thirty until nine. After that time, although I was there, only one car passed me around two o'clock, but I don't know if the driver saw me or not. At six the milk delivery man will tell you I was still there."

"I'm only interested in knowing where you were between one and four this morning."

"I was outside 33 Connaught Boulevard."

He shrugged his shoulders.

"Just to keep the record straight, let me see what you have in your pockets."

I turned out my pockets, laying the odds and ends on the desk. He watched without interest.

"If I had stolen her virtue," I said, "I wouldn't be carrying it around in my pocket."

He got to his feet.

"Don't leave town. I only need a puff of wind to throw you in the tank as a material witness, so watch yourself."

He walked out of my office, through the outer room and into the passage. He left both doors wide open.

I collected my possessions and returned them to my pockets, then I pushed the door shut and sat on my desk and lit a cigarette. Right now they hadn't a watertight case against me, but they did have something. A lot depended on what they turned up within the next few hours. Although Retnick was a bird-brain, I had a feeling the killer was framing me for the murder and would drop another clue in front of Retnick that could be a clincher. The disappearance of my gun could only mean the killer had shot her with it and it might turn up where Retnick would find it.

I slid off the desk. This wasn't the time to sit around shaking my head at myself. I had work to do.

I locked up the office and headed for the elevator. Against Jay Wayde's glass-panelled door, I saw Retnick's shadow. He was talking to Wayde, collecting evidence against me.

With a sense of urgency, I rode down to the ground floor, walked by the two cops at the door, then crossed the street to where I had left my car.

I got in and slammed the door.

I was now as jittery as a junkie. I had a sudden urge for a slug of whisky. Drinking before six o'clock wasn't my usual routine, but this was something special. I slid across the bench seat and opened the glove compartment. As I reached for the bottle, my heart gave a big kick against my ribs and my mouth turned as dry as a sun-bleached bone.

In the glove compartment lay my .38 police special and a lizard skin handbag.

I sat staring, feeling a chill crawl up my spine. As sure as I was breathing, this handbag belonged to the dead Chinese woman.

3

At the back of police headquarters there is a large yard surrounded by an eight foot high wall. Here, the police park their patrol cars, the riot squad trucks and the fast cars that rush experts to any emergency.

On one of the walls is a big notice that says in large red letters against a white background this park is for police vehicles only.

I swung my car through the open gateway and parked carefully beside a patrol car. As I cut the engine, a cop appeared from nowhere, his red Irish face showing violent fury.

"Hey! What's the matter with you? Can't you read?" he bawled in a voice that could be heard two blocks away.

"Nothing's the matter with me," I said as I removed the key

from the ignition, "and I can read—even the long words."

I thought he was going to explode. For a long moment he opened and shut his mouth while he struggled to frame words violent enough for the occasion.

Before he could give utterance, I said, smiling at him through the open window of my car, "Detective Lieutenant Retnick, the Mayor's brother-in-law, told me to park here. Take it up with him if you feel badly about it, but don't blame me if you get yourself kicked humpbacked."

He looked as if he had suddenly swallowed a bee. For two long seconds he glared at me, his mouth working, then he stalked away.

I sat staring into space for perhaps twenty minutes, then a car came into the yard and parked within ten feet of me. Retnick got out and started towards a door that led into the grey stone building that was police headquarters.

"Lieutenant . . ."

I didn't raise my voice but he heard me. He looked over his shoulder at me. He stiffened as if someone had goosed him with a branding iron, then he came over fast.

"What do you imagine you are doing here?" he demanded.

"Waiting for you," I said.

He considered this, staring intently at me.

"Well, I'm here—now what?"

I got out of the car.

"You searched me, Lieutenant, but you forgot to search my car."

He became very still, breathing heavily through his pinched nostrils, his hard watchful eyes alert.

"Why should I search your car, shamus?"

"You wanted to know what the yellow skin, as you call her, had in her handbag that had tempted me to shoot her in my office with my gun. You didn't find it in my office nor in my pockets. I should have thought a really keen cop would have checked my car to make sure I hadn't hidden the motive for murder there. So I've brought the car along just in case you wanted to be a really keen cop."

His face tightened with fury.

"Listen, you son-of-a-bitch," he mouthed. "I don't take smart talk from a cheap peeper. I'll get Pulski to handle you! He'll take the shine off your wit! You're too goddam smart to stay in one piece!"

"Better look in the car first before you feed me to your meat grinder, Lieutenant. Look in the glove compartment. It'll save time." I stepped away from the car, letting the car door swing open.

His eyes smouldering, Retnick leaned into the car and yanked open the glove compartment.

I watched his reactions. His fury died. He didn't touch either the gun or the handbag. He looked for a long moment, then turned to me.

"Is that your gun?"

"Yes."

"Her handbag?"

"It adds up, doesn't it?"

He studied me, puzzled.

"What the hell's this? You ready to make a statement admitting you killed her?"

"I'm laying the cards face up as they're dealt to me," I said. "I can't do more than that. It's up to you what you make of it."

He bawled to the cop guarding the gate. When the cop came over, Retnick told him to get Pulski fast.

While we waited, Retnick again looked at the gun and the handbag without touching them.

"I wouldn't give two bits for your chance of survival now, shamus," he said. "Not two bits."

"I wouldn't give two bits myself if I hadn't come here to show you what I found," I said, "but since I've come, I'll gamble two bits but no more."

"Do you always lock your car?" he asked, staring at me as his brain creaked into action.

"Yes, but I have a duplicate key in the drawer where I keep my gun. I didn't look but I bet it isn't there now."

Retnick scratched the side of his face with a rasping sound.

"That's right. When I looked for the gun, I didn't see any key."

Pulski came pounding across the yard.

"Give this car the works," Retnick said to him. "Check everything. Careful how you handle the gun and the handbag. Better let Lacey look at the gun. Get moving."

He nodded to me and we walked across the yard, up the three steps, through the doorway into a dimly-lit white-tiled passage that smelt the way all cops houses smell.

We tramped down a corridor, up a flight of stairs, down a corridor and into a room the size of a hen coop. There was a desk, two chairs, a filing cabinet and a window. It was as cosy and as comfortable as an orphanage's common room.

Retnick waved me to an upright chair while he eased his way around the desk and sat in the chair behind it.

"This your office?" I asked interested. "I'd have thought you being the Mayor's brother-in-law, they would have fitted you up with something more plush."

"Never mind how I live: concentrate on your own misfortunes," Retnick said. "If that's the gun that killed her and that's her handbag, you're as good as dead."

"Do you think so?" I said, trying to make myself comfortable on the upright chair. "You know for ten minutes, maybe even longer, I struggled against the temptation of ditching the gun

21

and the handbag in the sea and if I had ditched them, Lieutenant, neither you nor all the bright boys who take care of the law in this city would have been any the wiser, but I decided to give you a break."

"What do you mean by that?"

"I didn't ditch them because they had been so obviously planted in my car. It all adds up to a plant—the whole set-up. If I had ditched them, you might not be able to break the case."

He cocked his head on one side: he was good at doing that.

"So I have the gun and the handbag: what makes you think I'm going to break this goddam case?"

"Because you're not going to concentrate on me, you're going to look for the killer and that's what he doesn't want you to do."

He brooded for a long moment, then he took out his cigar case and offered it to me. This was his first friendly act during the five years I had known him. I took a cigar to show I appreciated the gesture although I am not by nature a cigar smoker.

We lit up and breathed smoke at each other.

"Okay, Ryan," he said. "I believe you. I'd like to think you knocked her off, but it's leaning too far backwards. I'd be saving myself a hell of a lot of trouble and time if I could believe it, but I can't. You're a cheap peeper, but you're not a fool. Okay, so I'm sold. You're being framed."

I relaxed.

"But don't count on me," he went on. "The trouble will be to convince the D.A. He's an impatient bastard. Once he knows what I've got on you, he'll move in. Why should he care so long as he gets a conviction?"

There didn't seem anything to say to that so I didn't say it.

He stared out of the window that gave onto a view of the back of a tenement building with badly washed laundry hanging on strings and baby carriages on balconies.

"I've got to dig around before I can make up my mind about you," he said finally. "I can book you as a material witness or I can ask you to stick around voluntarily. What's it to be?"

"I'll stick around," I said.

He reached for his telephone.

"I want you," he said when a voice sounded over the line.

There was a pause, then the door pushed open and a young plain-clothes man came in. He was the eager-beaver type. I could see, so far, police work hadn't soured him. He looked at Retnick the way a friendly dog looks for a bone.

With an expression of distaste, as if he were introducing a poor relation, Retnick waved to me.

"This is Nelson Ryan: a shamus. Take him away and keep him amused until I want him." He looked at me. "This is Patterson. He's just joined the force: don't corrupt him faster than he need be."

22

I went with Patterson down the corridor and into another small room that smelt of stale sweat, fear and disinfectant. I sat down by the window while Patterson, looking puzzled, squatted on the edge of a desk.

"Relax," I said. "We'll probably be here for hours. Your boss is trying to prove I murdered a Chinese woman and he hasn't a chance to prove it."

His eyes bugged out as he stared at me.

Trying to put him at ease, I offered him the half-smoked cigar Retnick had given me. "This is a museum piece. Would you like to have it for your collection? It's Retnick's. You have a museum?"

His young, eager face turned to stone. He looked almost like a cop.

"Listen, let me tell you something. We don't like . . ."

"Yeah, yeah, yeah," I said, waving my hand to cut him short. "I've heard that one before. Retnick tells it better. I stir up the dust. I get in your way. I bother you boys. Okay, so what? I make a living the same as you. Can't I kid you a little or are you that sensitive?"

I grinned at him, and after a moment's hesitation, he relaxed and grinned back. From then on we got along fine.

Around lunch-time a cop brought us a meat pie and some beans which we ate. Patterson seemed to think the pie was pretty good, but then he was young and hungry. I toyed with mine and sent most of it back. After this so-called lunch, he got out a deck of cards and we played gin rummy for matches. After I had taken a whole box off him, I showed him how I was cheating him. This seemed to shock him until I offered to teach him how it was done. He made a very enthusiastic pupil.

Around eight o'clock the same cop brought more meat pie and more beans. We ate the stuff because by now we were so goddam bored we would have eaten anything just for the hell of it.

We played more gin rummy and he cheated so well he took a whole box of matches off me. Around midnight, the telephone bell rang. He picked up the receiver, listened, then said, "Yes, sir," and hung up. "Lieutenant Retnick is ready for you now," he said, getting to his feet.

We both felt the way people feel when the train at last steams out of the station and they can stop talking the way people talk when seeing people off at a station.

We went down the corridor to Retnick's office.

Retnick was sitting at his desk. He looked tired and worried. He waved me to a chair and waved Patterson away. When Patterson had gone, I sat down.

There was a long pause as we stared at each other.

"You're a lucky guy, Ryan," he said eventually. "Okay, I didn't think you killed her, but I was goddam sure the D.A. would have thought so if I'd turned you over to him. Now I can persuade him you didn't do it. Consider yourself a lucky son-of-a-bitch."

I had been in this building for fifteen hours. There had been times when I had wondered if I had played my cards right. I had had moments of near-panic, but now hearing what he said, I relaxed, drawing in a deep breath.

"So I'm lucky," I said.

"Yeah." He slid down in his chair and groped for a cigar. Then realising he had a dead one between his teeth, he took it out, sneered at it and dropped it into the trash-basket. "I've had practically the whole of the force working on this thing for the past fourteen hours. We've turned up a witness who saw you in your car at two-thirty this morning on Connaught Boulevard. The witness happens to be an attorney who hates the D.A.'s guts and he had his wife with him. His evidence would blow a great big hole in any case the D.A. might have cooked up against you. So, okay, you didn't kill her."

"Would it be nosey to ask if you have any idea who did kill her?"

He offered me his cigar case: this time I could afford to refuse. As he put the case back in his pocket, he said, "It's too early yet. Whoever he is, he's played it neat. No clues: no nothing so far."

"Didn't you get a line on the Chinese woman?"

"Oh, sure, that wasn't hard. There was nothing but the usual junk a woman carries in the handbag, but we got her spotted at the airport. She came from Hong Kong. Her name is Jo-An Jefferson. Believe it or not, she's the daughter-in-law of J. Wilbur Jefferson, the oil millionaire. She married the son, Herman Jefferson, in Hong Kong about a year ago. He was recently killed in a car smash and she brought his body back for burial."

"Why?" I asked, staring at him.

"Old man Jefferson wanted his son buried in the family vault. He paid this girl to come over with the body."

"What's happened to the body?"

"It was picked up at the airport by a mortician at seven o'clock this morning, acting on orders. It's at his parlour waiting interment."

"You checked that?"

He yawned, showing me half his false teeth.

"Listen, shamus, you don't have to tell me my job. I've seen the coffin and inspected the papers: everything's in order. She flew in from Hong Kong, arriving here at one-thirty. She took a taxi from the airport to your office block. What beats me is why she came to see you immediately she arrived and how her killer knew she was coming to see you. What did she want with you?"

"Yeah. If she was from Hong Kong, how would she know I existed?" I said.

"Your idea she telephoned for an appointment around seven after you had left your office is out. She was in the air at that time. If she had written, you would have known about it."

I thought for a moment.

"Suppose Hardwick met her at the airport? He called me from the airport at six. Suppose he waited for her to arrive and told her he was me. Suppose he went on ahead while she was clearing the coffin through the authorities and slipped the lock on the outer door. A lock isn't too hard to slip and then waited for her to join him.

He didn't seem to like this idea much: nor did I.

"But what the hell did she want with you?" he demanded.

"If we knew that we wouldn't be asking each other questions. How about her luggage? Did you locate it?"

"Yeah. She checked it in at the left-luggage office before leaving the airport: one small suitcase; nothing in it except a change of clothes, a small Buddha and some joss sticks. She certainly travelled light."

"Have you talked to old man Jefferson yet?"

He pulled a face.

"Yeah, I've talked to him. He acted as if he hated my guts. I think he does. That's the hell of marrying into an influential family. My brother-in-law and Jefferson get along like I get along with a boil on my neck."

"Still it has its compensations," I said.

He fingered his pearl stick-pin.

"Sometimes. Anyway, the old goat didn't let his hair down. He said he wanted me to catch the man who had killed his daughter-in-law, otherwise there would be trouble." He stroked his beaky nose. "He draws a lot of water in this city. He could make trouble for me."

"He wasn't helpful?"

"He certainly wasn't."

"How about the Express messenger who delivered the three hundred bucks to me? He could have seen the killer."

"Look, shamus, you're not half the ball of fire you think you are. I checked on him: nothing. But this is interesting: the envelope containing the dough was handed in at four o'clock at the Express headquarters which as you know is across the way from you. None of the dim-witted clerks can remember who handed it in, but the instructions were to deliver it to you at six-fifteen."

"You checked Herron Corporation to see if Hardwick works there?"

"Yeah. I've checked every goddam thing. He doesn't work for them." He yawned, stretched, then stood up. "I'm going to bed. Maybe tomorrow I'll strike something. Right now I've had enough of it."

I got up too.

"It was my gun that killed her?"

"Yeah. No prints: nothing on the car. He's a neat bird, but he'll make a mistake . . . they always do."

"Some of them."

He looked sleepily at me.

"I've done you a good turn, Ryan, you try to do me one. Any ideas you get, let me know. Right now I need ideas."

I said I wouldn't forget him. I went down to where I had left my car and drove fast back to my apartment and to my bed.

4

I got to the office the next morning soon after nine o'clock. I found a couple of newspaper men parked outside my door. They wanted to know where I had been all yesterday. They had been trying to get to me to hear my side of the murder story and they were irate they hadn't been able to find me.

I took them into my office and told them I had spent the day at police headquarters. I said I knew no more about the murder than they did, probably less. No, I had no idea why the Chinese woman had come to my office at such an hour nor how she had got into the building. They spent half an hour shooting questions at me, but it was a waste of their time. Finally, disgruntled, they went off.

I looked through my mail and dropped most of it into the trash-basket. There was a letter from a woman living on Palma Mountain who wanted me to find the person who had poisoned her dog.

I was typing her a polite letter telling her I was too busy to help her when there came a knock on my door.

I said to come in.

Jay Wayde, my next-door neighbour, came in. He looked slightly embarrassed as he came to rest a few feet from my desk.

"Am I disturbing you?" he asked. "It's not my business really, but I wondered if they had found out who killed her."

His curiosity didn't surprise me. He was one of those brainy types who can't resist mixing themselves up with crime.

"No," I said.

"I don't suppose it helps," he said apologetically, "but thinking about this, I remember hearing your telephone bell ring around seven o'clock. It rang for some time. That was after you had left."

"My telephone is always ringing," I said, "but thanks. Maybe it might help. I'll tell Lieutenant Retnick."

He ran his hand over his close-cropped hair.

"I just thought . . . I mean in a murder investigation every little thing can be important until it is proved otherwise." He moved restlessly. "It's an odd thing the way she got into your office, isn't it? I guess it has been a bit difficult for you."

"She got into my office because the killer let her in," I said, "and it hasn't been difficult for me."

"Well, that's good. Did they find out who she was?"

"Her name is Jo-An Jefferson and she's from Hong Kong."

"Jefferson?" He became alert. "I know a friend named Herman Jefferson who went out to Hong Kong: an old school friend."

I tilted back my chair so I could put my feet on the desk.

"Sit down," I said. "Tell me about Herman Jefferson. The Chinese woman was his wife."

That really shook him. He sat down and gaped at me.

"Herman's wife? He married a Chinese?"

"So it seems."

"Well, I'll be damned!"

I waited, watching him.

He thought for a moment, then said, "Not that it shocks me. I've heard Chinese girls can be attractive, but I can't imagine his father would be pleased." He frowned, shaking his head. "What was she doing here?"

"She brought her husband's body back for burial."

He stiffened.

"You mean Herman's dead?"

"Last week . . . a car accident."

He seemed completely thrown off balance. He sat there, staring blankly as if he couldn't believe what he had heard.

"Herman . . . dead! I'm sorry," he said at last. "This will be a shock to his father."

"I guess so. Did you know him well?"

"Well, no. We were at school together. He was a reckless fella. He was always getting into trouble: fooling around with girls, driving like a madman, but I admired him. You know how kids are. I looked on him as a bit of a hero. Then later, after I had gone through college, I changed my views about him. He didn't seem to grow up. He was always drinking and getting into fights and raising general hell. I dropped him. Finally, his father got tired of him and shipped him out East. That would be some five years ago. His father has interests out there." He crossed one leg over the other. "So he married a Chinese girl. That certainly is surprising."

"It happens," I said.

"He died in a car accident? He was always getting into car smashes. I wonder he lasted as he did." He looked at me. "You know to me this is damned intriguing. Why was she murdered?"

"That's what the police are trying to find out."

27

"It's a problem, isn't it? I mean, why did she come here to see you? It really is a mystery, isn't it?"

I was getting a little bored with his enthusiasm.

"Yeah," I said.

Through the wall, I heard a telephone bell start ringing. He got to his feet.

"I'm neglecting my business and wasting your time," he said. "If I can remember anything about Herman that I think might help, I'll let you know."

I said I'd be glad and watched him leave, closing the door after him.

I sank lower in my chair and brooded over what he had told me. I was still sitting there, twenty minutes later, still brooding and still getting nowhere when the telephone bell jerked me out of my lethargy. I scooped up the receiver.

"This is Mr. J. Wilbur Jefferson's secretary," a girl's voice said: a nice, clear voice that was easy to listen to. "Is that Mr. Ryan?"

I said it was.

"Mr. Jefferson would like to see you. Could you come this afternoon at three o'clock?"

I felt a sharp stirring of interest as I opened my date book and surveyed its blank pages. I had no appointment for three o'clock this afternoon: come to that, I had no appointment for any day this week.

"I'll be there," I said.

"It is the last house, facing the sea on Beach Drive," she told me. "Beach View."

"I'll be there."

"Thank you."

She hung up.

I held the receiver against my ear for a brief moment while I tried to recapture the sound of her voice. I wondered what she looked like. Her voice sounded young, but voices can be deceptive. I hung up.

My morning passed without incident. I envied Jay Wayde whose telephone seemed to be constantly ringing. I could also hear the continuous clack-clack of a typewriter. He was obviously a lot busier than I, but then I had the mysterious Mr. Hardwick's three hundred dollars to keep me from starving anyway for a couple of weeks.

No one came near me, and around one o'clock I went down to the Quick Snack Bar for the usual sandwich. Sparrow was busy so he couldn't bother me with questions, although I could see he was itching to be brought up to date on the murder. I left with the rush hour still in full swing, aware of his reproachful expression as I left without telling him anything.

Later, I drove out to Beach Drive, the lush-plush district of

Pasadena City. Here, rich retired people lived with their own private beaches, away from the crowds that invaded the city during the summer months.

I reached the gates of Beach View a few minutes to three o'clock. They stood open as if I were expected and I drove up a forty-yard drive, bordered on either side by well-kept lawns and flower-beds.

The house was over large and had an old-fashioned air. Six broad white steps led up to the front entrance. There was a hanging bell-pull and the front door was of fumed oak.

I pulled the chain and after a minute or so, the door opened. The butler was a tall gloomy-looking old man who stared impassively at me; raising one busy eyebrow inquiringly.

"Nelson Ryan," I said. "I'm expected."

He moved aside and motioned me into the dark hall full of heavy dark furniture. I followed him down a passage and into a small room containing a few uncomfortable looking chairs and a table on which lay some glossy magazines: a room that had the atmosphere of a dentist's reception-room. He indicated one of the chairs and went away.

I stood around for about ten minutes, looking out of the window at the view of the sea, then the door opened and a girl came in.

She was around twenty-eight to thirty, slightly taller than average: dark, nice to look at without being sensational. Her eyes were slate blue, intelligent and remote. She had on a dark blue dress that merely hinted of her well shaped body. The neckline was severe and the skirt length modest.

"I'm sorry to have kept you waiting, Mr. Ryan," she said. Her smile was slight and impersonal. "Mr. Jefferson is ready for you now."

"You are his secretary?" I asked, recognising the clear, quiet voice.

"Yes. I'm Janet West. I'll show you the way."

I followed her out into the passage and through a green baize door into a big old-fashioned but comfortable lounge lined with books and with double windows opening onto a secluded walled garden full of standard rose trees that were giving of their best.

J. Wilbur Jefferson was reclining on a bed-chair, fitted with wheels. He lay in the shade just outside the double windows: an old man, tall, thin and aristocratic with a big hooked nose, skin as yellow as old ivory, hair like white spun glass and thin fine hands heavily veined. He was wearing a white linen suit and white buckskin shoes. He turned his head to look at me as I followed Janet West into the garden.

"Mr. Ryan," she said, drawing aside and motioning me forward, then she went away.

"Use that chair," Jefferson said, pointing to a basket chair close to him. "My hearing isn't as good as it was so I'll ask you to keep your voice up. If you want to smoke . . . smoke. It's a vice I have been forced to give up now for more than six years."

I sat down, but I didn't light a cigarette. I had an idea he might not like cigarettes. When he had smoked, he would have smoked cigars.

"I've made inquiries about you, Mr. Ryan," he went on after a long pause while his pale brown eyes went over me intently, giving me the feeling he was looking into my pockets, examining the birthmark on my right shoulder and counting the money in my wallet. "I am told you are honest, reliable and not without intelligence."

I wondered who could have told him that, but I put my modest expression on my face and didn't say anything.

"I have asked you here," Jefferson went on, "because I would like to hear first-hand this story of the man who telephoned you and how, later, you found this Chinese woman dead in your office."

I noted he didn't call her his daughter-in-law. I noted too that when he said 'this Chinese woman', his mouth turned down at the corners and there was distaste in his voice. I guess for a man as old and as rich and as conventional as he, the news that your only son has married an Asian could come as a jar.

I told him the whole story, remembering to keep my voice up.

When I had finished, he said, "Thank you, Mr. Ryan. You have no idea what she wanted to see you about?"

"I can't even make a guess."

"Nor have you any idea who killed her?"

"No." I paused then added, "The chances are this man who calls himself John Hardwick did it or at least he is implicated."

"I have no confidence in Retnick," Jefferson said. "He is a brainless fool who has no right to his official position. I want the man who murdered my son's wife caught." He looked down at his veined hands, frowning. "Unfortunately, my son and I didn't get along well together. There were faults on both sides as there usually are, but I realise now that he is dead that I could have been much more tolerant and patient with him. I believe my lack of tolerance and my disapproval of his behaviour goaded him to be wilder and more reckless than he would have been if he had been more understood. The woman he married has been murdered. My son wouldn't have rested until he had found her murderer. I know his nature well enough to be sure of this. My son is dead. I feel the least I can do now is to find his wife's murderer. If I succeed, I shall feel I have squared my account with him to some extent." He paused and looked across the garden, his old face hard and sad. The slight breeze ruffled his white hair. He looked very old but very determined. He turned to look at me. "As you can see, Mr. Ryan, I am an old man. I am burnt out. I get tired easily. I am in no physical shape to hunt down a murderer and that is why I have sent for you. You are an interested party. This woman was found in your office. For some reason the murderer has tried to shift the responsibility onto you. I intend to pay you well. Will you find this man?"

It would have been easy to have said yes, taken his money and then waited hopefully to see if Retnick would turn up the killer, but I didn't work like that. I was pretty sure I didn't stand a chance of finding the killer myself.

"The investigation is in the hands of the police," I said. "They are the only people who can find this man—I can't. A murder case is outside an investigator's province. Retnick doesn't encourage outsiders stirring up the dust. I can't question his witnesses. It would get back to him and I would land in trouble. As much as I would like to earn your money, Mr. Jefferson, it just wouldn't work."

He didn't seem surprised, but he looked as determined as ever.

"I understand all that," he said. "Retnick is a fool. He seems to have no idea how to set about solving this case. I suggested he should cable the British authorities in Hong Kong to see if we can find out something about this woman. We don't know anything about her except she married my son and was a refugee from Red China. I know that because my son wrote about a year ago telling me he was marrying a Chinese refugee." Again he looked across the garden as he said, "I foolishly forbade the marriage. I never heard from him again."

"Do you think the British police will have information about her?" I asked.

He shook his head.

"It is possible, but not likely. Every year more than a hundred thousand of these unfortunate refugees come into Hong Kong. They are stateless people with no papers. I have a number of contacts in Hong Kong and I try to keep up to date with the situation. As I understand it, it is this: refugees fleeing from Red China are smuggled by junk to Macau which, as you probably know, is Portuguese territory. Macau can't cope with the invasion nor do they wish to. The refugees are transferred to other junks sailing for Hong Kong. The British police patrol the approaches to Hong Kong, but the Chinese are patient and clever when they want to get their own way. If a junk carrying refugees is spotted by the police, the police boat converges on it, but there are hundreds of junks fishing the approaches to the island. Usually the refugee junk succeeds in mixing with the fishing junks that close protectively around it and since all junks look alike, it becomes impossible for the police boat to find it. I understand the British police are sympathetic towards the refugees: after all, they have had a horrible time and they are escaping from a common enemy. The search for them ceases once the junk succeeds in reaching

31

Hong Kong's territorial waters. The police feel that as these poor wretched people have got so far, it wouldn't be human to send them back. But all these people are anonymous. They have no papers. The British police supply them with new papers, but there is no means of checking even their names. From the moment they arrive in Hong Kong, they begin an entirely new life with probably new names: they are reborn. My son's wife was one of these people. Unless we can find out who she really was and what her background was, I doubt if we'll ever discover why she was murdered and who her murderer is. So I want you to go to Hong Kong and see if you can find out something about her. It won't be easy, but it is something Retnick can't do and the British police wouldn't be bothered to do. I think you can do it and I'm ready to finance you. What do you think?"

I was intrigued by the idea, but not so intrigued that I didn't realise it could meet with no success.

"I'll go," I said, "but it could be hopeless. I can't say what chances I have until I get out there, but right now, I don't think I have much of a chance."

"Go and talk to my secretary. She'll show you some letters from my son that may be helpful. Do your best, Mr. Ryan." He gave me a slight gesture of dismissal. "You will find Miss West in the third room down the passage to your right."

"You realise I can't go at once?" I said, getting to my feet. "I'll have to attend the inquest and I'll have to get Retnick's say-so before I leave."

He nodded. He seemed now to be very tired.

"I'll see Retnick doesn't obstruct you. Go as soon as you can."

I went away, leaving him staring stonily in front of him: a lonely man with bitter memories tormenting his conscience.

5

I found Janet West in a large room equipped like an office. She sat at a desk, a triple cheque book in front of her and a pile of bills at her elbow. She was writing a cheque as I entered the room. She looked up, her eyes probing. She gave me a slight smile which could have meant anything and indicated a chair by the desk.

"Are you going to Hong Kong, Mr. Ryan?" she asked, pushing the cheque book aside. She watched me as I sat down.

"I guess so, but I can't leave at once. I could make it by the end of the week if I'm lucky."

"You will need a smallpox shot. Cholera too would be wise, but it isn't compulsory."

"I'm all up to date with my shots." I took out a pack of cigarettes, offered it and when she shook her head, I lit up and put the pack back in my pocket. "Mr. Jefferson said you had some letters from his son. I need every scrap of information I can get, otherwise it'll be just so much waste of time going all that way."

"I have them ready for you."

She opened a drawer and took out about six letters which she handed to me.

"Herman only wrote once a year. Apart from the address I'm afraid they won't tell you much."

I glanced through the letters: they were very short. In each one was an urgent request for money. Herman Jefferson was no correspondent, but he certainly seemed to have had money on his mind. He merely stated he was in good health and he wasn't having any luck and could his father let him have some money as soon as he could. The first letter was dated five years ago and each letter was written at yearly intervals. The last letter, however, did interest me. It was dated a year ago.

> *Celestial Empire Hotel,*
> *Wanchai.*
>
> Dear Dad,
> *I've met a Chinese girl and I'm marrying her. Her name is Jo-An. She has had a tough life as she is a refugee from China, but she's pretty, smart and my type of woman. I guess you won't be exactly pleased with my news, but you've always said I must lead my own life so I'm marrying her. I'm satisfied she'll make me a good wife. I'm looking around for an apartment but it is not easy as prices come high. We may decide to stay on here at the hotel. It is convenient in some ways although I prefer to have a home of my own.*
> *I hope you will send us your blessing. If you feel like sending a cheque towards an apartment it would be very welcome.*
>
> > *Yours ever,*
> > *Herman.*

I laid down the letter.

"That was the last letter he wrote," Janet West said quietly. "Mr. Jefferson was very angry. He cabled, forbidding the marriage. He heard nothing more from or about his son until ten days ago when this letter arrived."

She handed over a letter written on cheap notepaper which smelt faintly of sandalwood. The writing was badly formed and not easy to read.

> *Celestial Empire Hotel,*
> *Wanchai.*
>
> Mr. Jefferson,
> *Herman died yesterday. He had a car crash. He often said he wanted to be buried at home. I have no money but if you will*

*send me some I will bring him back so he can be buried the way
he wanted to be. I have no money to bury him here.*

Jo-An Jefferson.

This struck me as a pathetic letter and I imagined this Chinese
girl suddenly left alone with the unburied body of her husband,
without money and without any future unless her father-in-law
relented and took pity on her.

"Then what happpened?" I asked.

Janet West rolled her gold fountain pen across the blotter. Her
remote eyes went a shade more remote.

"Mr. Jefferson wasn't satisfied this letter was genuine. He
thought possibly this woman was trying to get money out of him
and that his son wasn't dead. I telephoned the American Consul
at Hong Kong and learned that Herman had died in a motor
accident. Mr. Jefferson then told me to write to this woman, telling
her to send the body back. He suggested she should remain in
Hong Kong and he would arrange an income to be paid regularly
to her, but as you know, she came back with the body, although
she didn't come here."

"And the body?"

I had a sudden idea that she was controlling herself. I could
sense the tension in her although it didn't show.

"The funeral will be the day after tomorrow."

"Just what did Herman do in Hong Kong for a living?"

"We don't know. When he went there first, his father arranged
for him to have the position of assistant manager to an export
firm but after six months, Herman left. Since then, he never told
his father what he was doing: only these yearly requests for
money."

"Did Mr. Jefferson give him what he asked for?"

"Oh yes. Whenever he was asked, he always sent money."

"From these letters," I said, touching the letters, "Herman
seems to have asked for money once a year. Were the sums sub-
stantial?"

"Never more than five hundred dollars."

"He couldn't have lived on that for a year. He must have earned
something besides."

"I suppose so."

I rubbed my jaw while I stared out of the window, my mind
busy.

"There's not much to go on, is there?" I said finally. Then I
asked the question I had been wanting to ask since I had become
aware of her nearly-concealed tension. "Did you know Herman
Jefferson personally?"

That got a reaction. I saw her stiffen slightly and the remoteness
went out of her eyes for a brief moment, but came back.

"Why, yes, of course. I have been with Mr. Jefferson for eight

34

years. Herman lived here before he went out East. Yes: I knew him."

"What sort of man was he? His father says he was wild but he now thinks if he had been more understanding his son wouldn't have been so wild. Do you agree?"

Her eyes flashed suddenly and I was startled to see how hard she could look when she let her mask slip.

"Mr. Jefferson was very shocked to learn his son was dead," she said, her voice sharp. "At the moment he is feeling sentimental. Herman was vicious, callous and amoral. He was a thief. He stole money from his father: he even stole money from me. It is hard to believe he was Mr. Jefferson's son. Mr. Jefferson is a fine man: he has never done a mean thing in his life!"

I found her intensity slightly embarrassing.

"Well, thanks," I said and got to my feet. "I'll do my best for Mr. Jefferson, but I'll have to have some luck."

She flicked through a pile of signed cheques, found one and pushed it across the desk.

"Mr. Jefferson wishes to pay you a retainer. I will have your air ticket ready when you let me know when you can leave. If you need more money, please let me know."

I looked at the cheque. It was signed by her and for a thousand dollars.

"I'm not this expensive," I said. "Three hundred would have been enough."

"Mr. Jefferson told me he wanted you to have it," she said as if she had handed me five bucks."

"Well, I never refuse money." I looked at her. "You handle Mr. Jefferson's affairs?"

"I'm his secretary," she said, a curt note in her voice.

"Well . . ." There didn't seem anything to say to that, so instead, I said, "I'll contact you as soon as I know when I can leave."

As I was moving to the door, she said, "Was she very pretty?"

For a moment I didn't catch on, then I looked quickly at her. She sat still, and there was a curious expression in her eyes I couldn't read.

"His wife? I guess so. Some Chinese women are very attractive. She was—even in death."

"I see."

She picked up her fountain pen and pulled the triple cheque book towards her. It was her way of dismissing me.

I found the butler waiting for me in the hall. He let me out with a slight bow. No one could ever accuse him of being over talkative.

I walked slowly to my car. That last scrap of dialogue had been enlightening. I was suddenly sure at one time or the other Janet West and Herman Jefferson had been lovers. The news of his marriage and his death must have been as great a shock to her as

35

it had been to old man Jefferson. This was an unexpected and interesting development. I decided it might pay off to know something more about Janet West.

I got into my car and drove to police headquarters. I had to wait half an hour before I could see Retnick. I found him at his desk, chewing a dead cigar and in a depressed mood.

"I don't know if I want to waste time with you, shamus," he said as I shut the door and came over to his desk. "What do you want?"

"I'm now employed by J. Wilbur Jefferson," I said. "I thought you should know."

His face hardened.

"If you foul up my investigation, Ryan," he said, "I'll see you lose your licence. I'm warning you." He paused, then went on, "What's he paying you?"

I sat down on the upright chair.

"Enough. I won't have a chance to foul up anything. I'm going to Hong Kong."

"Who wouldn't be a peeper," he said. "Hong Kong, eh? Wouldn't mind going there myself. What do you imagine you'll do when you get there?"

"The old man wants to know who the girl is. He thinks we won't get anywhere until I've dug up her background and taken a look at it. He could be right."

Retnick fidgeted with a ball pen for some moments, then he said, "It'll be a waste of money and time, but I don't suppose that'll worry you as long as you get paid."

"It won't," I said cheerfully. "He can afford to indulge his whims and I can afford the time. I might even strike lucky."

"I know as much about her as you'll ever find out. I didn't have to go to Hong Kong to find out either. All I had to do was to send a cable."

"And what did you find out?"

"Her name was Jo-An Cheung—that's a hell of a name, isn't it? Three years ago she was caught landing in Hong Kong from a junk from Macau. She spent six weeks in jail and was then given papers. She worked as a taxi dancer at the Pagoda Club and that probably means she was a prostitute." He scratched his ear, looking out of the window for some moments before going on. "She married Jefferson before the American Consul on the 21st of September of last year. They lived together at a Chinese joint called the Celestial Empire Hotel. Jefferson seems to have had no work. He probably lived on what she earned and what he picked up from his old man. On September 6th of this year, he was killed in a car smash and she applied to the American Consul for permission to take his body back to his home. That's the story. Why go to Hong Kong?"

"I'm being paid to go. Anyway, I'll be out of your way."

36

He grinned evilly. "Don't worry about getting in my way, shamus. I can get you out of my way any time."

I gave him that. There were times when he had to feel important: this was one of them.

"Well, how's the case going? Getting anywhere?"

"No." He scowled down at his ink-stained blotter. "What foxes me more than anything is why she came to your office at three o'clock in the morning."

"Yeah. Maybe I'll get the answer in Hong Kong." I paused to light a cigarette, then went on, "Old man Jefferson is worth a lot of money. I imagine his son would have inherited it. Unless his father altered his Will, Jo-An would have been his heiress now the son is dead. Someone might have been tempted to knock her off so she didn't inherit. I'd like to find out who is coming into his money now. Could be a motive for the murder."

He brooded, then said, "You get an idea now and then. Yeah: it's an idea."

"Have you run into his secretary: Janet West? It wouldn't surprise me if she doesn't pick up some of Jefferson's money when he passes on. I think, one time, she was in love with the son. Could be an idea to check where she was at three o'clock when the Chinese woman was shot."

"How do I do that?" Retnick asked. "I've met her. The old man is gaga about her. If I start digging into her private life, I could run into trouble and that's something I never do. He draws a lot of water in this town." He looked hopefully at me. "What makes you think she was in love with the son?"

"I've been talking to her. She has a nice line of control, but it slipped a little. I'm not suggesting she killed the girl, but maybe she knows more about the killing than she lets on. Maybe she has an ambitious boy friend."

"I'm not going to chase that goat," Retnick said. "What I've got to find out is why that yellow skin came to your office. Once I find that out, the case is solved."

I got to my feet.

"You could be right. When is the inquest? I'd like to get off as soon as I can."

"Tomorrow at ten. It won't mean a thing, but you'll have to be there." He poked the ball pen into his blotter. "Don't forget, if you turn up anything, I want to know."

"Don't you do anything for your pay?"

He made a sour face.

"Who calls it pay? I have to watch my step. Jefferson draws . . ."

"I know . . . you told me."

I left him digging more holes in his blotter. The killer of Jo-An Jefferson would have liked to have seen him. The sight would have given him a lot of confidence.

I returned to my office. As I was about to unlock my door, I had

37

an idea. I walked the few yards down the corridor and knocked on Jay Wayde's door, then pushed it open.

I walked into a large office, well furnished, with a desk facing the door on which stood a tape recorder, a telephone, a portable typewriter and a couple of steel 'In and Out' trays.

Wayde sat behind the desk, smoking a pipe, pen in hand, papers before him.

There was another door to his right. Through it came the clack-clack of a busy typewriter.

The office had a much more prosperous air than mine, but being an industrial chemist was a much more paying racket than being a private investigator.

"Hello there," Wayde said, obviously pleased to see me. He half rose to his feet, waving to a leather lounging chair by his desk. "Come on in and sit down."

I came on in and sat down.

"This is unexpected." He looked at his gold Omega. "How about a drink? It's close on six. Will you have a Scotch?"

He seemed so anxious to act the host, I said I would have a Scotch. He hoisted a bottle and two glasses out of a drawer and poured large snorters into the glasses. He apologised for not having ice. I said I was used to slumming and would survive. We grinned at each other and drank. It was pretty good Scotch.

"What you told me about Herman Jefferson interested me," I said. "I was wondering if you could give me some more information. I'm coasting around. Any angle would be helpful."

"Why, sure." He looked the way a St. Bernard dog might look when it hears a cry of distress. "What angle had you in mind?"

I gave him my puzzled I-wish-I-knew expression I use when dealing with types like Jay Wayde.

"I don't know," I said. "My job is to collect as many facts as I can in the hope they'll make sense. For instance, you knew Jefferson. You told me something about his character. You said he was reckless, a bit of a drunk, got into fights and generally raised hell. How was he with women?"

Wayde's sun-tanned face showed sudden righteous indignation. I could guess how he was with women. His sex impulses would be worked out of his system with a golf club.

"He was rotten with women. Okay, when you are young, you fool around with girls—I fooled around myself, but Herman was plain rotten. If his father hadn't had so much influence in this city, there would have been endless scandals."

"Any girl in particular?" I asked.

He hesitated, then said, "I don't like mentioning names, but there was this girl, Janet West. She's Mr. Jefferson's secretary. She . . ." He paused and his eyes shifted from mine. "Look, excuse me, I don't think I should talk about this. After all, it happened

38

nearly nine years ago. I know because Herman told me, but that doesn't give me the right to tell you."

I could see he was longing to tell me: longing to participate in a murder hunt and feeling pretty important that I was interested in what he had to tell.

So I said gravely, "Every scrap of information I can get might lead me to the killer. You should ask yourself if you have the right not to tell me."

He loved that. His eyes brightened and he leaned forward, staring earnestly at me.

"Well, of course, putting it like that, I see what you mean." He ran his hand over his crew-cut and then putting on an expression of a virtuous man who has no truck with scandal, he said, "Herman and Janet West had an affair about nine years ago. There was a baby. Herman ducked out of it and she went to his father who was horrified. The baby died. The old man insisted that Herman should marry the girl, but Herman flatly refused. I think the old man rather fell for her himself. Anyway, he took her into his home and made her his secretary. Herman told me about it. He was mad that his father should bring the girl into his home. I guess the old man hoped Herman would have a change of heart and marry her, but when finally the nickel dropped and he realised Herman wasn't going to, he fixed for Herman to go East. Janet has been with the old man ever since."

"She's attractive," I said. "I'm surprised she hasn't married."

"It doesn't surprise me. The old man wouldn't like it. He depends on her, and after all, there is no one else for him to leave his millions to now Herman's dead."

"There isn't?" I tried to conceal my interest. "He must have some relations."

"No. I used to know the family pretty well. Herman told me he would inherit as there were no other claimants. I bet Janet will pick up quite a tidy slice when the old man goes."

"Pretty lucky for her Herman's wife can't claim it."

He looked startled.

"I hadn't thought of that angle. Not much chance. I can't imagine the old man would have left a Chinese woman anything."

"As Herman's wife, she could make a claim. If the judge was sympathetic, she could have got away with it."

The door on the right opened and a girl came in with a pile of letters to be signed. She was the kind of girl I would expect Wayde to employ: mousey, scared and with glasses.

I got up as she put the letters on the desk.

"I must run along," I said. "Be seeing you."

"Are there any further developments?" he asked as the girl left the room. "Have the police got any clues?"

"Not a thing. The inquest is for tomorrow, but they'll have to bring in a verdict of murder by persons unknown. It was a pretty neat killing."

"I'll say." He drew the letters towards him. "If there is anything I can do . . ."

"I'll let you know."

Back in my office, I called Retnick and told him what I had learned about Janet West.

"The ball is in your court," I said. "If I were you, I'd want to know where Miss West was at three o'clock when the Chinese woman died."

There was a pause while I listened to his heavy breathing.

"But then you aren't me," he said finally. "See you at the inquest. Don't forget to put on a clean shirt. The coroner's a fussy son-of-a-bitch," and he hung up.

6

As I had anticipated, the inquest went off without any fuss or excitement. A fat keen-eyed man who introduced himself to Retnick as Jefferson's attorney sat at the back, but didn't contribute anything to the proceedings. Janet West, looking pretty and efficient in a dark tailor-made, told the coroner more or less what she had told me. Retnick said his piece and I said mine. The inquest was adjourned for the police to make further inquiries. I had the feeling that no one was particularly interested that a Chinese refugee had been murdered.

When the coroner had left the court, I went over to Retnick who was gloomily poking a match amongst his teeth.

"Okay for me to leave town now?" I asked.

"Oh, sure," he said indifferently. "Nothing to keep you here." He looked slyly at Janet West, who was talking to Jefferson's attorney. "Did you find out if she was in bed when the yellow skin got hers?"

"I'll leave that to you," I said. "Now's the time when she has an attorney with her. Step right up and ask her."

He grinned, shaking his head.

"I'm not that crazy," he said. "Have a good time. Watch out for the Chink girls. From what I hear they're not only willing but wanton."

He went off, giving Janet West and the attorney a wide berth. I hung around until the attorney had gone, then as Janet West was moving towards the exit, I joined her.

"I can get off tomorrow," I said as she paused and looked at me with her quizzing remote eyes. "Any chance of a plane reservation?"

"Yes, Mr. Ryan. I'll have your ticket this evening. Is there anything else you want?"

"I'd like a photograph of Herman Jefferson. Can you fix that?"

"A photograph?" She seemed surprised.

"It could be useful. I'm getting a morgue shot of his wife. Photos are always useful when on a job like this."

"Yes: I can get you one."

"How would it be if we met somewhere down town this evening? It'll save me driving out to your place. I've got a lot to do before I go. Suppose we say at the Astor Bar at eight?"

She hesitated, then nodded.

"Yes: then at eight."

"Thanks: it'll help a lot."

She nodded again, gave me a cool little smile and walked away. I watched her get into a two-seater Jaguar and drive away.

Don't moon over her, sucker, I said to myself. If she's coming into Jefferson's millions, she'll find someone a lot more interesting than you: and that wouldn't be so hard either.

I drove to the office and spent the rest of the morning tidying up the various outstanding odds and ends. Luckily, I had nothing on hand that mattered: nothing that couldn't wait a couple of weeks, but I hoped I wouldn't have to be away that long.

I was just thinking of going over the way for a sandwich when a tap came on the door and Jay Wayde wandered in.

"I won't keep you," he said. "I wanted to know the time of Herman's funeral. Do you know? I think I should be there."

"It's tomorrow," I said, "but I don't know the time."

"Oh." He looked disconcerted. "Well, maybe I could call Miss West. I wonder if they would mind if I went?"

"I'm seeing Miss West this evening. I'll ask her if you like."

"I wish you would." He brightened up. "It's a bit embarrassing for me to ask. I mean I haven't seen him for so long. It just occurred to me . . ." He let the sentence drift away.

"Sure," I said.

"How did the inquest go?"

"As I thought: it's been adjourned." I paused to light a cigarette. "I'm off to Hong Kong tomorrow."

"You are?" He looked a little surprised. "That's quite a trip. Something to do with this business?"

"Sure. Old man Jefferson's hired me to look into the girl's background. He's paying: so I'm going."

"Is that a fact? You know that's one of the places I'd really like to visit. I envy you."

"I envy myself."

"Well, I'll be interested to hear how you get on." He shifted from one foot to the other. "Think you'll find out anything?"

"I haven't an idea. I can but try."

"So you met Mr. Jefferson. How did you find him?"

41

"Not so hot. He doesn't look as if he's going to last long."

"I'm sorry to hear that. He's pretty old." He shook his head. "Must have been a jolt to him when Herman went." He began to move to the door. "Well, I only looked in. I have someone coming to see me. Have a good trip. Anything I can do for you while you're away?"

"Not a thing, thanks. I'll lock up and that'll be that."

"Well, then I'll be seeing you. We'll have a drink together on your return. I'll be interested to hear how you get on and what you think of the place. You won't forget about the funeral? You might ask if one can send flowers."

"I'll let you know tomorrow."

Later in the afternoon, I drove over to police headquarters and picked up the morgue photo of Jo-An Jefferson that Retnick had promised me. It was a good photograph. By letting the light fall on her dead eyes, the photographer had given her a resemblance of life. I sat in my car for some minutes, studying the picture. She had been certainly attractive. I had asked the morgue attendant what the funeral arrangements were. He told me she was to be buried at Jefferson's expense at the Woodside Cemetery the day after tomorrow. That meant she wasn't being put away in the family vault. The Woodside Cemetery was not for the lush-plush residents of Pasadena City.

Around six o'clock, I locked up the office and went home. I packed a bag: did the various things one has to do when leaving for a couple of weeks, took a shower, shaved, put on a clean shirt, then drove down town to the Astor Bar, arriving there at five minutes to eight.

Janet West arrived as the minute hand of my strap watch shifted to the hour. She came in with that confident air a well-dressed, good-looking woman has who knows she looks good and is pleased about it.

Male heads turned to watch her as she made her way to the corner table where I was sitting. We said the usual things polite strangers say to each other when meeting and I ordered her a vodka martini while I had a Scotch.

She gave me the airplane ticket and a leather wallet.

"I got some Hong Kong dollars for you," she said. "It'll save you the trouble at the other end. Would you want me to telephone for a room for you? The Peninsular or the Mirama are the best hotels."

"Thanks, but I'm aiming to stay at the Celestial Empire."

She gave me a quick alert stare as she said, "Yes, of course."

"Did you remember the photograph?"

As the waiter set the drinks, she opened her lizard handbag and gave me an envelope.

The half-plate glossy print was obviously a professional job. The man photographed was staring intently at the camera. There was a sly, half grin in his eyes: not a pleasant face. Dark, with thick black eyebrows, coarse featured, a strong ruthless jaw line, a thin mouth. The kind of face you would expect to see in a police line-up.

I was surprised. I wasn't expecting Herman Jefferson to look like this. I had in mind a more easy-going, irresponsible, playboy type. This man could do anything that was violent and vicious, and do it well.

I remembered what she had said about him. 'He was utterly and thoroughly bad. He had no redeeming feature.' Looking at this man's face, I could accept this statement now.

I looked up. She was watching me: her face expressionless, but her eyes were cold.

"I see what you mean," I said. "He doesn't take after his father, does he?"

She didn't say anything to that but continued to watch me as I put the photograph in my wallet. I had a sudden idea for no reason at all and I took out the morgue shot of Jo-An.

"You asked me if she was pretty," I said. "Here she is," and I offered the photograph.

For a long moment she made no move to take the photograph. Maybe the light was deceptive, but I had an idea she lost colour. Her hand was steady enough as she finally took the photograph. It was now my turn to watch her as she studied the dead woman's face. She stared for a long moment, her face expressionless. I wondered what was going on in her mind. Then she handed me back the photograph.

"Yes," she said, her voice cold and flat.

I picked up my glass and she picked up hers. We drank.

"You said the funeral was tomorrow?" I asked.

"Yes."

"A friend of Herman's asked me to find out the time and if he could go. He has an office next to mine. His name is Jay Wayde. He went to school with Herman."

She stiffened.

"Only Mr. Jefferson and I are attending the service," she said. "None of Herman's friends would be acceptable."

"I'll tell him. He wanted to send flowers."

"There are to be no flowers." She looked at her watch, then got to her feet. "Mr. Jefferson is expecting me. I must get back. Is there anything else I can do for you?"

We had scarcely touched our drinks. I was vaguely disappointed. I had hoped to have got to know her better, but it was like trying to talk to someone behind a nine foot wall.

"No, thanks. What time does the plane take off?"

"Eleven o'clock. You should be at the airport at half past ten."

"Thanks for fixing it." As she began to move towards the exit,

I hurriedly shoved two dollars at the waiter and followed her out onto the street.

The Jaguar was parked exactly opposite the bar. I had had to drive around two blocks three times before I had finally found parking room about a couple of hundred yards away. That proved either she or more probably old man Jefferson had plenty of pull in this city.

She paused by the car.

"I hope you have a successful trip," she said. There was no smile. Her eyes were still remote. "If there is anything you think of you need before you leave, please telephone me."

"Don't you ever relax?" I asked, smiling at her. "Do you never take time off from being an efficient secretary?"

Just for a brief moment there was a flicker of surprise in her eyes, but it was quickly gone.

She opened the door of the car and got in. It was neatly done: there was no show of knees. She slammed the door shut before I could put my hand on it.

"Good night, Mr. Ryan," she said, and stabbing the starter button, she slid the car into the traffic and was away.

I watched the car out of sight, then looked at my strap watch. The time was thirty-five minutes past eight. I would have liked to have had her as a companion for dinner. The evening stretched ahead of me: empty and dull. I stood on the edge of the kerb and thought of the four or five girls I knew who I could call up and have dinner with, but none of them were in Miss West's bracket: none of them would amuse me this night. I decided to eat another goddam sandwich and then go home and watch television.

I wondered what Jay Wayde would have thought if he knew I was planning to spend this kind of evening. He would probably have been shocked and disillusioned. He would have expected me to have been at some clip-joint talking tough to a blonde or wrestling rough with some redhead.

I walked into a snack bar. The juke-box was blaring swing. Two girls in jeans and skin-tight sweaters were perched on stools at the bar, their round little bottoms pushed out suggestively, their hair in the Bardot style, their grubby fingers red-tipped.

They looked at me as I came in, their hard worldly young eyes running over me speculatively, then they looked away. Too old, too dull and obviously no fun.

I ate a beef and ham sandwich, feeling depressed. Even going to Hong Kong in the morning failed to light a spark. I took out the photographs of Herman and Jo-An and studied them. They made an ill-assorted pair. The man worried me. I couldn't understand how a girl like Janet West had not only fallen for him but had produced his baby.

I thought the hell with it and put the photographs away. Then

44

paying for the sandwich, I went out onto the street, aware the two girls were staring after me. One of them laughed shrilly. Maybe she thought I was funny to look at. I didn't blame her. There were times when I was shaving I thought so too.

I drove back to my top-floor apartment that consisted of a reasonably large living-room, a tiny bedroom and an even tinier kitchen. I had lived there ever since I had come to Pasadena City. It was central, cheap and convenient. It had no elevator, but I didn't worry about that. Walking up five flights of stairs kept my figure in trim and kept anyone but a good friend away.

I was panting slightly by the time I reached my front door. As I fumbled for my key, I told myself I'd better cut down on the cigarettes, but I knew I was just kidding myself.

I unlocked the door and walked into my living-room. I didn't see him until I had shut the door. The room was very dim: it was dusk and he was in black.

There was a big neon sign advertising a soap powder across the way and its gaudy blue, green and red tubes made a reflection on the ceiling. If it hadn't been for the sign, I wouldn't have seen him at all.

He was sitting in my best armchair that had been moved close to the window. He sat with his legs crossed, his hands on a folded newspaper on his lap and he seemed relaxed and at ease.

He certainly gave me a shock that set my heart thumping.

The light switch was just by me. I snapped it on.

He wasn't much more than a kid: around eighteen or nineteen, but powerfully built with thick lumpy shoulders. He had on a black greasy leather jacket, a black woollen cap with a dirty red tassel, black corduroy trousers and a black cotton handkerchief knotted at his thick throat.

You can see the type any night hanging around in gangs outside bars: a typical product of the streets: as vicious and as dangerous as a cornered rat.

His skin was the colour of cold mutton fat. His eyes were the flat, glittering eyes of a muggle smoker and a killer. His right ear was missing and he had a thick white scar of an old knife wound running along his jaw line. He was the most terrifying looking specimen of a delinquent I had ever seen.

He scared the hell out of me.

He gave me a cold, sneering grin.

"Hi, Buster, I thought you were never coming," he said in a hoarse, rasping voice.

I thought of my gun somewhere at police headquarters. I was getting over the shock now, but I would have been a lot happier if I had had the gun under my coat.

"What the hell are you doing in here?" I said.

"Relax, Buster: squat. I got business with you." He waved to a chair. I saw he was wearing black cotton gloves and that brought

45

me out in a sweat. I knew this young punk was lethal and he could be lethal to me. He was too confident: much, much too confident. I looked closely at him. The pupils of his eyes were enormous. He was junked to the tassel of his woollen cap.

"I'll give you two seconds to get out of here before I throw you out," I said, forcing my voice to sound tough.

He sniggered, rubbing the tip of his waxy-looking nose with a gloved finger. He shifted his legs and the newspaper slid onto the floor. I saw the .45 resting on his thighs. It had a twelve-inch metal tube screwed into the barrel.

"Squat, Buster," he said. "I know you ain't got a rod." He tapped the extension tube. "It's silent. I made this hicky myself. It'll last for three shots, but one'll be plenty."

I looked at him and he looked at me, then moving slowly, I sat down, facing him. There were six feet of carpet between us. From this distance I could smell him. He smelt of dirt, stale sweat and reefer smoke.

"What do you want?" I demanded.

"You tired of life, Buster?" he asked, making himself more comfortable by shifting his thick body in the chair. "You'd better be. You ain't got long to live."

Looking into those flat, drugged eyes that were as impersonal as the eyes of a snake sent a chill up my spine.

"I like life," I said for the sake of something to say. "I get along fine with it."

"Too bad." He moved the gun slightly so that the black tube was suddenly pointing directly at me. "You got a girl?"

"Several—why?"

"Just wondered. Will they be sad when they hear you've been knocked off?"

"One or two might. Look, this is a crazy conversation. What have you against me? What have I done to you?"

"Not a thing, Buster." His thin bloodless lips curled into a sneering smile. "You look a nice guy. You got a nice apartment. I watched you arrive. You got a nice car."

I drew in a long, deep breath.

"Suppose you put that gun away and let's get pally," I said without much hope. "How about a drink?"

"I don't drink."

"Good for you. There are times when I wish I didn't. I could do with a drink right now. Would that be all right with you?"

He shook his head.

"This isn't a drinking party."

While this insane conversation was going on, my mind was busy. He was big and strong and tough. If it wasn't for the gun, I would have been ready to take him. I'm not all that weak myself and I've learnt a trick or two to take care of a punk his weight

46

and build. I was within six feet of him. One quick jump would put me on equal terms with him if it wasn't for the gun.

"What kind of party is it then?" I asked, moving my right foot so that it was slightly behind the front leg of my chair. In that position I had the correct leverage to catapult myself at him if I got the chance.

"Shooting party, Buster," he said and sniggered.

"Who's getting shot?"

"You are, Buster."

I wished I wasn't sweating so hard. It irritated and bothered me. I've been in tight spots before, but none quite so tight as this one. I wished I wasn't feeling so goddam cowardly. "But why? What's it all about?"

He lifted the gun and rubbed the hole where his ear should have been with the barrel of the gun.

"I don't know. I don't care either," he said. "I'm just making some easy dough."

I licked my lips. My tongue was so dry it was a waste of an effort.

"You getting paid to shoot me? Is that it?"

He cocked his head on one side.

"Why sure, Buster. Why else should I want to shoot you?"

"Tell me about it," I said in a strangled voice. "We've got lots of time. Who's paying you to shoot me?"

He shrugged his lumpy shoulders indifferently.

"I wouldn't know, Buster. I was playing pool when this jerk comes up and asks me if I'd like to make five hundred bucks. We got in a corner and he gives me a hundred and he tells me to come here and put a slug into you. When I've done it, he'll give me the rest of the dough. So here I am."

"Who was this guy?"

"I don't know: just a guy. Where would you like to have it, Buster? I'm good with this rod. A brainshot is the quickest, but you please yourself."

"What did this guy look like?" I said desperately.

He scowled and lifted the gun so it was pointing at my head.

"You don't have to worry about him," he said, and there was a sudden savage note in his voice. "You start worrying about yourself."

"Five hundred isn't so much. I could top it," I said. "How about putting that gun away and I pay you a thousand?"

He sneered at me.

"When I make a deal, I stick to it," he said.

Then the telephone bell rang.

For the past twenty seconds I had been bracing myself. The bell startled him and he looked towards the telephone.

I launched myself at him, the top of my head aimed at his face, my hands for the gun.

47

I hit him like a rocket: my head smashing into his mouth and nose. My hands closed over the gun, wrenching it aside as it went off with a sound no louder than a bursting paper bag.

He and I and the chair went over backwards with a crash that shook the room.

But he was tough all right. I couldn't get the gun out of his hand. He had a grip like a vice. He was partially stunned, otherwise he would have nailed me, but I had time to roll over and hit him on the side of his thick neck with a chopping blow that slowed him down. His grip loosened and I got the gun. Then he hit me between the eyes with the heaviest punch I'd ever walked into. It was like being hit with a hammer.

I let go of the gun. For a brief moment all I could see were flashing lights dancing before my eyes. I was crawling to my knees as he pushed himself off the floor, blood streaming from his nose and mouth. He aimed a kick at my face, but there was no steam in it. I had hurt him, and when a junkie like him gets hurt, he stays hurt.

I blocked the kick with my arm, rolled away from him and somehow stood up. We faced each other. The gun lay on the floor between us.

He snarled at me, but he was smart enough not to bend for the gun. He knew I would nail him before he reached it: instead he came at me like a charging bull. I got in one solid punch to his face as he thudded into me and then we both crashed against the wall, bringing down two water-colours of Rome I had picked up out there when on an assignment and had carted home for the memory.

I used my head in his face again and slammed six fast punches into his belly, taking two swings to the head that made my brain reel. He drew back. Those punches in his belly had softened him. He was looking wild-eyed now. I jumped him, hitting him again. He swerved aside and then I saw the knife in his hand.

We paused and stared at each other. He was in one hell of a mess. My head had mashed his features and his face was a mask of blood, but he was still a killer. The look in his eyes and the knife in his hand rattled me.

I backed away from him.

He snarled at me and began to creep forward.

My shoulders hit the wall. I pulled off my coat and with one quick movement wrapped it around my left arm. He came at me then as fast and as viciously as a striking snake. I caught the knife thrust on my padded arm and socked him on the side of his jaw with my right fist. It was a good, explosive punch. The whites of his eyes showed and he reeled back, sagging at the knees. The knife slipped out of his thick fingers. I kicked it across the room, then as I set myself, he began to fall forward. I hung a punch on his jaw again that ripped the skin off my knuckles. He went down with a thud, scraping his chin on the carpet.

I leaned against the wall, panting. I felt like hell. I had taken some of the heaviest punches I've ever taken and they had done something bad to me. It was as if some of my life had been drained out of me.

The door burst open and two cops stormed in, guns in hand.

You can't stage this kind of fight in my kind of apartment without alerting the whole block.

As they came in, the punk rolled over on his side. He had fallen on his gun and now it was in his hand. He was still trying to earn his money. He took a snap shot at me and I felt the slug fan my face before it made a hole in the wall, bringing down a shower of plaster.

One of the cops fired. I yelled at him, but it was too late.

The punk died, still trying for a second shot at me. He was conscientious if nothing else.

CHAPTER TWO

1

THE fat man, sweat beads on his balding head, leaned forward to look out of the window as the 'No Smoking' sign flashed up.

"Well, here we are—Hong Kong," he said over his shoulder. "Looks pretty good. They say there's no place quite like it on earth. Could be they are right."

As his big head was cutting off my view, I busied myself with my safety-belt. Finally when he leaned back to fix his own belt, I managed to catch a glimpse of green mountains, the sparkling blue sea and a couple of junks before we were bumping gently along the runway.

The fat man who had been my companion from Honolulu, reached up to collect a camera and a Pan-Am overnight bag.

"Are you staying at the Peninsula?" he asked me.

"I'm on the other side."

His sweating face showed disapproval.

"Kowloon's better: better shops: better hotels, but maybe you're here on business?"

"That's right," I said.

The explanation seemed to satisfy him.

The other passengers in the aircraft began to collect their hand luggage. The usual polite pushing and shoving went on for a while before I could squeeze myself out into the hot sunshine.

It had been a good trip, slightly over-long, but I had enjoyed it.

Ten minutes later, I was through the Customs and out into the noisy, bustling approach to the airport. I saw my fat companion being whisked away in a tiny hotel bus. He waved to me and I waved back. Half a dozen or so rickshaw boys converged on me, shouting and waving anxiously. Their old, yellow, dried up faces were imploring. As I stood hesitating, a broad, squat Chinese, neatly dressed in a city suit, came over to me and gave me a little bow.

"Excuse me, please," he said. "Perhaps I can help you? You would like a taxi?"

"I want to get to the Celestial Empire Hotel at Wanchai," I said.

"That will be on the island, sir." He looked slightly surprised in a polite way. "It would be best to take a taxi to the ferry and cross to Wanchai. The hotel is close to the ferry station on the other side."

"Thanks a lot," I said. "Will the driver speak English?"

"Most of them can understand a little English." He signalled to a taxi at the head of the rank. "If you will permit me. . . ."

He went on ahead. I picked up my bag and went after him. He spoke to the driver in what was probably Cantonese. The driver, a lean dirty-looking Chinese, grunted, glanced at me, then away.

"He will take you to the ferry, sir," the squat man said. "The fare will be one dollar: not an American dollar, you understand, but a Hong Kong dollar. As you will probably know there are approximately six Hong Kong dollars to the American dollar." He beamed at me. Every tooth in his head seemed to be capped with gold. "You will have no trouble in finding the hotel on the other side. It is opposite the ferry station." He hesitated, then added apologetically, "You know this particular hotel is scarcely for American gentlemen? Forgive the interference, but most American gentlemen prefer to stay at the Gloucester or the Peninsula. The Celestial Empire is for Asians."

"Yeah, but that's where I'm staying," I said. "Thanks for your help."

"You are welcome, sir," he said, and taking a limp wallet from his pocket, he presented me with his card. "You may need a guide. It is my business to take care of American gentlemen when they visit Hong Kong. You have only to telephone. . . ."

"Thanks. I'll remember that." I tucked the card under the strap of my wrist watch, then as he stepped back, bowing, I got into the taxi.

On the flight over I had boned up on Hong Kong, discovering the mainland where the Kai Tak airport is situated is called the Kowloon Peninsula and across the Straits is the island of Hong Kong, reached by fast ferry-boat service in four or five minutes.

Wanchai, where Jefferson had lived, was a waterfront district of Hong Kong.

The drive to the ferry took only a few minutes. The Kowloon waterfront teemed with jog-trotting humanity. There seemed to be about only one European to every hundred Chinese: the scene reminded me of a disturbed ants' nest. Coolies, carrying fantastic burdens slung on thick bamboo poles, trotted in and out of the traffic, oblivious of the risk of being run down. Big American cars, driven by fat, sleek Chinese businessmen, rickshaw boys dragging crates and odd looking merchandise in their two-wheeled chariots and heavy trucks crowded the broad street. Gay red signs in Chinese lettering decorated the shop fronts. Small, dirty Chinese children with babies strapped to their backs played in the gutters. Chinese families squatted on the sidewalk outside their shops, shovelling rice into their mouths with chop sticks.

At the ferry, I paid off the taxi, bought a ticket at the turnstile and got on the ferry-boat that was already crowded with Chinese business men, American tourists and a number of pretty Chinese girls wearing Cheongsams, slit either side to show off their shapely legs.

I got a seat by the rail and as the ferry-boat churned through the blue waters of the Straits towards the island of Hong Kong, I tried to orientate myself to my new surroundings.

It seemed a long time since I had left Pasadena City. My journey had been delayed a couple of days because of my murderous visitor. I hadn't told Retnick the whole story. I had told him I had walked into my apartment, found the punk there and had started a fight. What he was doing there, I lied, I had no idea —probably a sneak-thief. Retnick didn't like it. Particularly, he didn't like the silencer on the gun, but I stuck to my story and got away with it. At least, I was able to leave for Hong Kong and that was all I was worrying about.

I was pretty sure the man who had hired the punk to kill me had been the mysterious John Hardwick. I had bought another .38 Police special. I told myself I mustn't move without it in the future: something I promised myself, but quickly forgot.

The ferry-boat bumped against the landing-stage and everyone, including me, crowded off.

Wanchai was nearly one hundred per cent Chinese. Apart from two burly American sailors who were chewing gum and staring emptily into space, the waterfront was given up to jog-trotting Chinese, coolies staggering under impossible burdens, vegetable vendors squatting on the kerb, Chinese children minding Chinese babies, a dozen or so young Chinese girls who stared at me with inviting, shrewd black eyes and the inevitable rickshaw boys who sprang into life at the sight of me.

Sandwiched between a shop selling watches and a shop selling cheap toys was the entrance to the Celestial Empire Hotel.

Lugging my bag, I managed to cross the road without getting run down and toiled up the steep, narrow stairs leading to the tiny hotel lobby.

Behind the counter at the head of the stairs sat an elderly Chinese wearing a black skull cap and a black tunic coat. Long straggly white hairs came from his chin. His almond-shaped eyes were as dull and as impersonal as black crepe.

"I want a room," I said, setting down my bag.

He eyed me over, taking his time. I wasn't wearing my best suit and my shirt had suffered during the flight. I didn't look like a bum, but I didn't look a great deal better.

He produced a dog-eared paper bound book which he offered me together with a ball-point pen. The book contained nothing but Chinese characters. I wrote my name and nationality in the required spaces and gave him back the book and the pen. He then lifted a key from a rack and handed it to me.

"Ten dollars," he said. "Room Twenty-seven."

I gave him ten Hong Kong dollars, took the key and as he waved his hand to the right-hand side of the narrow passage, I set off, lugging my bag. Half-way down the passage, a door opened and a thin, white American sailor, his cap set at a jaunty angle, stepped out in front of me. There was no room to pass so I turned sideways and waited. Behind him came a stocky Chinese girl wearing a pink Cheongsam, a bored expression on her flat face. She reminded me of a well-fed Pekinese dog. The sailor brushed past me, winking. The girl went after him. I walked on down the passage until I came to room twenty-seven. I sank the key into the lock, opened up and walked into a ten foot by ten foot room with a double bed, an upright chair, a cupboard, a wash-bowl standing on a set piece of white painted furniture, a strip of worn carpet and a window giving onto a view of another building that was possibly a laundry, judging by the towels, sheets and odd underwear drying on bamboo poles projecting from the windows.

I put down my bag and sat on the hard bed. I was sweating and feeling grimy. I would have liked to have been at the Gloucester or the Peninsular where I could have had a *de luxe* shower and an ice cold beer, but this was business. I hadn't come this far to indulge in luxury. This was where Herman Jefferson and his Chinese wife had lived. If it had been good enough for them, it would have to be good enough for me.

After a while, I began to sweat less. I poured water into the cracked bowl and had a wash. Then I unpacked and put my stuff away in the cupboard. The hotel was very quiet. I could just hear the murmur of distant traffic, but nothing else. I looked at my strap watch. The time was twenty minutes to six. I saw the card the squat Chinese had given me tucked under the strap and I pulled it out and read the inscription. It said: *Wong Hop Ho. English speaking guide.* There was a telephone number. I put the card in my wallet, then opening the door, I stepped into the passage.

A Chinese girl was leaning against the door-post of the room opposite. She was small, compactly and sturdily built: her glistening black hair was done up in a thick bun at the back of her neck. She was wearing a white blouse and a close-fitting bottle green skirt. She was nice to look at without being sensational. She was looking directly at me as if she had been waiting patiently for some time for me to appear.

"Hello, mister," she said with a wide, nice smile. "I'm Leila. What is your name?"

I liked her smile and I liked her dazzling strong white teeth.

"Nelson Ryan," I said, closing my door and turning the key. "Just call me Nelson. Do you live here?"

"Yes." Her friendly black eyes ran over me. "Few American gentlemen ever stay here. Are you staying here?"

"That's the idea. Have you been here long?"

"Eighteen months." She had a peculiar accent. I had to concentrate to understand what she said. She stared at me with that stare that meant what she meant. "When you want to make love, will you come and see me?"

I was fazzed for a moment, then I managed a smile.

"I'll remember, but don't depend on it."

A door farther up the passage opened and a fat little man who could be either Italian or French came out. He hurried by me, not looking at me. He was followed by a very young Chinese girl. I didn't think she could have been more than sixteen, but it is hard to judge with these people. She gave me a hard, interested stare as she passed me. I was now under no illusion about the kind of hotel I had landed myself in.

Leila put her beautifully shaped hands under her tiny breasts and lifted them.

"Would you like to come to me now?" she asked politely.

"Not right now," I said. "I'm busy. Some other time perhaps."

"American gentlemen are always busy," she said. "Tonight perhaps?"

"I'll let you know."

She pouted.

"That really doesn't mean anything. You will either come or you won't."

"That's the idea," I said. "Right now I have things to do," and I went off down the passage to the lobby where the old Chinese reception clerk sat as stolid and as inevitable as Buddha.

I went down the stairs and out into the crowded, heat-ridden street. A rickshaw boy came running over to me.

"Police headquarters," I told him as I climbed into the chair.

He set off at a jog-trot. After we had travelled two or three hundred yards, I realised the mistake of taking such a vehicle. The big, glossy cars and the trucks had no respect for rickshaws. Any second I felt I was going to be squashed either by a truck or by an over-large American car. I was relieved when we finally pulled up outside the Hong Kong Central Police Station, surprised to find I was still in one piece.

After stating my business to the desk sergeant, I finally got shown into a small, neat office where a Chief Inspector with grey hair and a military moustache regarded me with impersonal eyes as he waved me to a chair.

I told him who I was and he then told me who he was. His name was MacCarthy and he spoke with a strong Scottish accent.

"Jefferson?" He tilted back his chair and picked up a much-used, much-battered Dunhill pipe. As he began to fill it, he went on, "What's all the excitement about? I've already dealt with an inquiry from Pasadena City about this man. What's he to you?"

I told him I was acting for J. Wilbur Jefferson.

"I want to get as much information about his son and his Chinese wife as I can," I said. "Anything you can tell me could be helpful."

"The American Consul could be more helpful," he said, lighting his pipe. He blew a cloud of expensive-smelling tobacco smoke towards me. "I don't know much about him. He was killed in a car crash. You've heard about that?"

"How did it happen?"

He shrugged.

"Driving too fast on a wet road. There wasn't much to pick up when we found him. He was wedged in the car which had gone up in smoke."

"No one with him?"

"No."

"Where was he going?"

MacCarthy looked quizzingly at me.

"I don't know. The accident took place about five miles outside Kowloon in the New Territories. He could be going anywhere."

"Who identified him?"

He moved slightly, showing a degree of controlled patience.

"His wife."

"Can you fill me in on his background? How did he earn his living?"

"I don't think I can." He took the pipe out of his mouth and stared at the smoking bowl. "He wasn't my headache fortunately. He kept clear of us. Out here we don't interfere with people unless they make a nuisance of themselves and Jefferson was

54

careful not to do that. Every so often we got word about him. He wasn't a desirable citizen. There isn't much doubt that he lived on the immoral earnings of his wife, but here again, we don't interfere with an American citizen if we can help it."

"Any angles on the girl?"

He puffed smoke and looked bored.

"She was a prostitute, of course. That is a problem we're trying to cope with, but it isn't easy. These refugee girls have great difficulty in earning a living: prostitution is the easiest way out for them. We are gradually cleaning up the city, but it is uphill work."

"I'm trying to find out why she was murdered."

He shrugged his shoulders.

"I can't help you there." He looked hopefully at a pile of papers on his desk. "I've given all the information I have about these two to Lieutenant Retnick. There's nothing more I can add."

I can take a hint as well as the next man. I stood up.

"Well, thanks. I'll nose around. Maybe I'll turn up something."

"I doubt it." He pulled the papers towards him. "If there's anything I can do. . . ."

I shook hands with him and went out onto the busy Queen's Road. The time was now half past six. The American Consulate would be closed: not that I had much hope of getting any useful information about Jefferson or his wife from them. If I was going to get the information I wanted I would have to rely on myself to do the digging, but where to begin for the moment foxed me.

I wandered around the town for an hour, looking at the shops and absorbing the atmosphere of the place and liking it a lot. I finally decided I could do with a drink and I made my way along the waterfront towards Wanchai. Here I found a number of small bars, each with a Chinese boy squatting outside who called to me, inviting me in with a leer and a wink.

I entered one of the larger establishments and sat down at a table away from the noisy juke-box. Half a dozen American sailors lounged up at the bar, drinking beer. Two Chinese business men sat near me, talking earnestly, a file of papers between them. Several Chinese girls sat on a bench at the back of the room, giggling and talking to one another softly with the twittering sound of birds.

A waiter came over and I asked for a Scotch and Coke. When he had served me, a middle-aged Chinese woman, wearing a fawn and green Cheongsam, appeared from nowhere and took the vacant chair opposite me.

"Good evening," she said, her hard black eyes running over me. "Is this your first visit to Hong Kong?"

"Yeah," I said.

"Do you mind if I keep you company?"

"Why no. Can I buy you a drink?"

She smiled: her teeth were gold-capped.

"I would like a glass of milk."

I waved to the waiter who seemed to know what to get for he nodded, went away and came back with a pint glass full of milk.

"The food here is good," she told me, "if you feel like eating."

"A little early for me. Don't you go for anything stronger than milk?"

"No. Are you staying at the Gloucester? It is the best hotel."

"So I've heard."

She eyed me speculatively.

"Would you like a nice girl? I have a number of very young and pretty girls. I have only to telephone and they will come here. You don't have to have any of them if you don't care for them. I will send for them, but they won't worry you. You have only to tell me if one of them pleases you and I will arrange everything."

"Thanks, but not right now. Do you have trouble in finding girls?"

She laughed.

"I have trouble in not finding them. There are too many girls in Hong Kong. What else can they do except entertain gentlemen? Hong Kong is full of pretty girls eager to make a little money."

The Celestial Empire Hotel was only two or three hundred yards from this bar. It seemed reasonable enough that if this woman controlled the local prostitutes, she might have known Jo-An.

"A pal of mine when he was here last year met a girl he liked very much," I said. "Her name was Jo-An Wing Cheung. I'd like to meet her. Do you know her?"

For a brief moment, her black eyes showed surprise. If I hadn't been watching closely I would have missed the quick change of expression. Then she was smiling, her thin amber-coloured fingers playing a tattoo on the table.

"Yes, of course I know her," she said. "She is a fine girl . . . very beautiful. You will like her very much. I could telephone her now if you like."

It was my turn to hide my surprise.

"Well, why not?"

"She is my best girl," the woman went on. "You wouldn't mind going to a hotel with her? She is living with her parents and she can't take gentlemen to her apartment. It would be thirty Hong Kong dollars for her and ten dollars for the room." She showed her gold-capped teeth in a smile. "And three dollars for me."

I wondered what old man Jefferson would say if I itemised these charges on my expense sheet.

"That's okay," I said, and it was my turn to smile at her. "But how do I know this girl is Jo-An? She could be someone else, couldn't she?"

"You make a joke?" she asked, looking intently at me. "She is Jo-An. Who else could she be?"

"That's right. I make a joke."

She got to her feet.

"I will telephone."

I watched her cross the room to where the telephone stood on the bar. While she was telephoning, one of the American sailors moved over to her and put his arm around her shoulders. She waved him to silence and he looked across at me and winked. I winked back. The atmosphere in the bar was friendly and easy. There was nothing furtive about this transaction. By the time the woman had replaced the receiver, everyone, including the waiters, knew I had ordered a girl and she was on her way. They all seemed genuinely happy about the event.

The woman talked to the sailor and then picked up the telephone receiver again. Business seemed to be getting brisk.

I finished my drink, lit a cigarette, then signalled to the waiter for a refill.

Two Americans in violent beach shirts, came and sat at a table away from mine. When the Chinese woman had finished telephoning she came over to me.

"She will be only ten minutes," she said. "I will let you know when she comes," and nodding she went over to the two Americans and sat with them. After a five-minute conversation she got up and went to the telephone again.

A little over a quarter of an hour later, the bar door pushed open and a Chinese girl came in. She was tall and well built. She was wearing a black and white tight-fitting European dress. A black and white plastic handbag dangled from a strap she had wound around her wrist. She was attractive, sensual and interesting. She looked at the Chinese woman who nodded towards her. The girl looked at me and smiled, then she crossed the bar, moving with languid grace while some of the American sailors whistled to her, grinning in a friendly way at me.

She sat down beside me.

"Hello," she said. "What is your name?"

"Nelson," I said. "What's yours?"

"Jo-An."

"Jo-An—what?"

She reached out and helped herself to one of my cigarettes from the pack lying on the table.

"Just Jo-An."

"Not Wing Cheung?"

She gave me a quick stare and then smiled. She had very beautiful white teeth.

"That is my name. How did you know?"

"A pal of mine was here last year," I said, knowing she was lying to me. "He told me to look you up."

"I'm glad." She put the cigarette between her painted lips and I lit it for her. "Do you like me?"

"Of course."

"Shall we go then?"

"Okay."

"Will you give me three dollars for Madame?"

I gave her three dollars.

The middle-aged Chinese woman came over, showing all her gold-capped teeth.

"You are pleased with her?"

"Who wouldn't be?"

She collected the three dollars.

"Come and see me again," she said. "I'm always here."

The girl who called herself Jo-An got up and sidled towards the exit. I went after her, nodding to the sailors. One of them made the letter 'O' with his finger and thumb and then pretended to swoon into the arms of his pals. I left them horsing around and moved out into the hot bustling night where the girl was waiting for me.

"I know a clean cheap hotel," she said.

"So do I," I told her. "I'm staying at the Celestial Empire. We'll go there."

"It would be better to go to my hotel." She gave me a sidelong look.

"We go to my hotel," I said, and taking her elbow in my hand, I steered her through the crowds towards the hotel.

She moved along beside me. She was wearing an expensive perfume. I couldn't place it, but it was nice. There was a thoughtful, faraway expression on her face. We didn't say anything to each other during the short walk. She mounted the sharp flight of stairs. She had an interesting back and nice long legs. She waved her hips professionally as she moved from stair to stair. I found myself watching the movement with more interest than the situation required.

The old reception clerk was dozing behind his barricade. He opened one eye and stared at the girl, then at me, then shut the eye again.

I steered her down the passage. Leila was standing in her open doorway, polishing her nails on a buffer. She looked the girl over and then sneered at me. I sneered back at her, opened my door and eased my girl through into the hot, stuffy little room.

I closed the door and pushed home the flimsy bolt.

She said to me, "Could you give me more than thirty dollars? I could be very nice to you for fifty."

She pulled a zipper on the side of her dress to show goodwill. She was half out of the dress before I could stop her.

"Relax a moment," I said, taking out my wallet. "We don't have to rush at this."

She stared at me. I took out Jo-An's morgue photograph and offered it to her. Her flat, interesting face showed suspicious bewilderment. She peered at the photograph, then she peered at me.

"What is this?" she asked.

"A photograph of Jo-An Wing Cheung," I said, sitting on the bed.

Slowly she zipped up her dress. There was now a bored expression in her black eyes.

"How was I to know you had a photograph of her?" she said. "Madame said you wouldn't know what she looked like."

"Did you know her?"

She leaned her hip against the bedrail.

"Is she all that important? I am prettier than she is. Don't you want to make love to me?"

"I asked if you knew her."

"No. I didn't know her." She moved impatiently. "May I have my present?"

I counted out five ten-dollar bills, folded them and held them so she could feast her eyes on them.

"She married an American. His name was Herman Jefferson," I said. "Did you know him?"

She grimaced.

"I met him." She looked at Jo-Ann's photograph again. "Why does she look like this . . . she looks as if she's dead."

"That's what she is."

She dropped the photograph as if it had bitten her.

"It is bad luck to look at dead people," she said. "Give me my present. I want to go."

I took out Herman Jefferson's photograph and showed it to her.

"Is this her husband?"

She scarcely glanced at the photograph.

"I am mistaken. I have never met her husband. May I have my present?"

"You just said you had met him."

"I was mistaken."

We stared at each other. I could see by the expression on her face I was wasting time. She didn't intend to tell me anything. I gave her the bills which she slipped into her handbag.

"There's more where that came from if you can give me any information about Jefferson," I said without any hope.

She started towards the door.

"I know nothing about him. Thank you for your present."

She slid back the bolt and with a jeering wave of her hips, she was gone.

I knew I had been taken for a ride, but as I was spending Jefferson's money, I was a lot less depressed than I would have been if it had been my own money.

2

Later, I got tired of lying on the bed and I decided to go somewhere to eat As I opened the bedroom door, I saw Leila, propping her body up against her door-post across the passage. She had changed into a scarlet and gold Cheongsam which gave her a very festive air. She had put a white cyclamen blossom in her hair.

"She didn't stay long," she said. "Why did you bring her here when I'm here?"

"It was strictly business," I said, closing the door and turning the key. "I just wanted to talk to her."

"What about?" she asked suspiciously.

"This and that." I looked her over. She was really a very attractive little thing. "How would you like to have dinner with me?"

Her face brightened.

"That is a very good idea," she said. She darted into her tiny bedroom, snatched up her handbag and joined me in the passage. "I will take you to a very good restaurant. I am very hungry. We will eat a lot of good food, but it won't cost you much." She started off down the passage to the head of the stairs. I followed her. We passed the reception clerk who was doing a complicated calculation with the aid of a bead calculator. His old yellow fingers flicked away at the beads with astonishing speed. He didn't look up as we went down the stairs.

I followed Leila's sturdy little back across the road to a taxi station.

"We will have to take a taxi to the Star Ferry," she said. "The restaurant where we will eat is on the mainland."

We picked up a taxi and drove to the Star Ferry, then we got on the ferry boat. During the trip over, she told me about a movie she had seen that afternoon. She said she went to the movies every afternoon. The Chinese, she explained, were very interested in the movies and they went as often as they could. From the queues I had seen outside every movie-house I could believe that. Leila said they began to queue at eleven in the morning to get the best seats.

When we reached the mainland, Leila suggested we should walk up Nathan Road. She said the exercise would sharpen her appetite.

It was not possible to walk two abreast and still more impossible to talk to her. At this hour the streets were crammed with people. Walking in the streets of Kowloon turned out to be quite an experience. Everywhere were glaring neon signs. Chinese characters, I decided, made the best and most interesting of any neon sign. They lost the vulgarity of a sign you can read and became works of art. Cars, rickshaws and bicycles swarmed along the broad street. The sidewalk was packed with a steady flow of humanity: all as active as ants.

We finally came to the restaurant in a side street which was crowded with children playing in the gutters, vegetable vendors packing up their wares for the night, parked cars and the inevitable blaze of neon signs.

"Here we eat very well," Leila said, and pushing open the swing door she entered the restaurant that emitted a noise like a solid punch on the ear—stunning and deafening.

We could see nothing of the diners. Every table was hidden behind high screens. The rattle of Mah Jongg tiles, the high-pitched excited Chinese voices and the clatter of dishes were overwhelming.

The owner of the restaurant opened two screens, bowing and smiling at Leila, and we were immediately submerged in noise and privacy.

Leila set her handbag down on the table, adjusted her brassière, shifted her solid little bottom firmly in her chair and showed me her beautiful white teeth in a radiant and excited smile.

"I will order," she said. "First, we will have fried shrimps, then we will have shark's fin soup, then we will have beggar chicken—it is the speciality here. Then we will see what else there is to eat, but first we commence with fried shrimps."

She spoke rapidly in Cantonese to the waiter and then when he had gone, she reached across the table and patted my hand.

"I like American gentlemen," she told me. "They have much vitality. They are very interesting in bed and they also have much money."

"Don't count on either of those statements," I said. "You could be disappointed. How long have you been in Hong Kong?"

"Three years. I came from Canton. I am a refugee. I only escaped because my cousin owns a junk. He took me to Macau and then I came here."

The waiter brought us Chinese wine. He poured it into two tiny cups. It was warm and reasonably strong. When he had gone, I said, "Maybe you know Jo-An Wing Cheung who is also a refugee."

She looked surprised.

"Yes. I know her very well. How do you know her?"

"I don't," I said.

There was a pause as the waiter set before us a bowl of king-size shrimps cooked in a golden batter.

"But you know her name. How do you know her name?" Leila asked, snapping up a shrimp with her chopsticks and dipping it in Soya sauce.

"She was married to a friend of mine who lived in my home town," I said, dropping a shrimp on the tablecloth. I nipped it up again with my uncertain chopsticks and conveyed it cautiously to my mouth. It tasted very good. "Did you ever meet him? His name's Herman Jefferson."

"Oh, yes." Leila was eating with astonishing speed. Three-quarters of the shrimps were gone before I could spear my third. "Jo-An and I escaped from Canton together. She was lucky to find an American husband even though now he is dead."

The waiter came with a bowl of fried rice in which was mixed finely-chopped ham, shrimps and scraps of fried egg. Leila filled her bowl and her chopsticks flashed as she whipped the food into her mouth. I lagged behind. To do justice to this meal, you had to have considerably more experience with chopsticks than I had.

"He lived with her at your hotel?" I asked as I dropped rice onto the tablecloth in a vain effort to keep pace with her.

She nodded.

The shrimps had disappeared and more than half the rice. She certainly had the technique of getting the most inside herself in the shortest time.

"He lived with her in a room next to mine for three months after they married, then he went away."

A large bowl of shark's fin soup appeared. Leila began to fill her bowl.

"Why did he go away?"

She shrugged her shoulders.

"He didn't need her any more."

As I could eat the soup with a spoon, I managed to keep pace with her.

"Why didn't he need her any more?"

Leila paused for a moment to give me a cynical stare, then she went on spooning soup into her small, insatiable mouth.

"He only married her so she could keep him," she said. "When he began to make money for himself, he didn't want her."

"How did she manage to keep him?" I asked, knowing what the answer would be.

"She entertained gentlemen as I do," Leila said, and looked serenely at me. "We have no other means of making money."

The waiter came through the screens. He brought with him a strip of matting which he laid ceremoniously on the floor.

Leila turned in her chair, clasping her small hands excitedly. "This is the beggar's chicken. You must not miss seeing any of this."

A Chinese boy came in carrying what appeared to be an enormous ostrich egg on a wooden plate. He rolled the egg onto the matting.

"The chicken is first rubbed with many spices and then wrapped in a covering of lotus leaves," Leila explained, squirming around on her chair with excitement. "It is then covered with clay and put on an open fire and cooked for five hours. You can see the clay has become as hard as stone."

The boy produced a hammer and cracked the egg open: from it came an aroma that was unbelievably delicious. The waiter and the boy squatted opposite each other. The boy eased the chicken out of the layers of lotus leaves onto the dish held by the waiter. The bird had been so thoroughly cooked the flesh fell from the bones as it unrolled onto the dish.

With skilled and enthusiastic hands, the waiter spooned pieces of the chicken into our bowls.

Leila's chopsticks began to flash again. I began on my portion. It was quite the most sensational dish I had ever eaten. Leila paused for a brief moment, a shred of chicken held securely in her chopsticks to ask, "You like?"

I grinned at her.

"Sure . . . I like."

There was no point in asking her further questions until the meal was over. I could see her concentration was now centred on the food and I didn't blame her. We finished the chicken, then she ordered mushrooms, bamboo shoots, salted ginger and finally almond cake. By this time I had given up. I sat, smoking a cigarette, marvelling at the amount of food she could put away. After a further twenty minutes, she laid down her chopsticks and heaved a long, satisfied sigh.

"It was good?" she said, looking inquiringly at me.

I regarded her with considerable respect. Anyone who could eat as much as she had and still keep a nice shape was entitled to respect.

"It was wonderful."

She smiled contentedly.

"Yes, it really was wonderful. May I please have a cigarette?"

I gave her a cigarette and lit it for her. She blew smoke from her small neatly made-up mouth and then her smile became inviting.

"Would you like to return to the hotel now?" she said. "We could make love. It would be good after such a meal."

"It's early yet . . . we have the night before us," I said. "Tell me more about Herman Jefferson. You say he began to make money three months after he married Jo-An. How did he make it?"

She frowned. I could see Jefferson as a subject bored her.

"I don't know. Jo-An didn't tell me. One day I found her

alone and crying. She said he had left her. He no longer needed her because he was now making money."

"She didn't tell you how?"

"Why should she? It wasn't my business."

"Did he come back?"

"Oh, he came back from time to time." Leila pulled a face. "Men come back when they want a change. He only came back for a night now and then."

"What did Jo-An do when he left her?"

"Do?" Leila stared at me. "What could she do? She worked as before."

"Entertaining gentlemen?"

"How else could she live?"

"But if Jefferson was making money and she was his wife, surely he gave her something?"

"He gave her nothing."

"Do you know where he lived after he left her?"

"Jo-An told me he had rented a big villa belonging to a Chinese gambler at Repulse Bay. I have seen the place." Leila heaved an envious sigh. "It is very beautiful . . . a big white villa with steps leading down into the sea with a little harbour and a boat."

"Did Jo-An ever go there?"

Leila shook her head.

"She was never asked."

The waiter came in smiling and bowing. He gave me the check. The price of the meal was ridiculously cheap. I paid while Leila watched with a happy expression on her face.

"You are pleased?" she asked.

"It was a wonderful meal."

"Let us go back to the hotel then and make love."

I was in Hong Kong. There was this odd atmosphere of surrender to the senses that made argument difficult. Besides, I had never made love to a Chinese girl. It was something I felt I should do.

"Okay," I said, getting to my feet. "Let us go back to the hotel."

We went out into the noisy dark night with the clatter of Mah Jongg tiles following us.

We began to walk down Nathan Road.

"Perhaps you would like to buy me a little present?" Leila said, taking my arm and smiling persuasively at me.

"I could be talked into it. What had you in mind?"

"I will show you."

We walked a little way, then she steered me into a brilliantly lit arcade of small shops. Before each shop stood a smiling, hopeful Chinese salesman.

"I would like to have a ring to remember you by," Leila said. "It need not be an expensive ring."

We went into a jewellers and she selected an imitation jade

64

ring. It wasn't much of a ring, but it seemed to delight her. The salesman asked forty Hong Kong dollars. Leila and he spent ten minutes haggling and finally she got it for twenty-five dollars.

"I will always wear it," she said, smiling at the ring on her finger. "I will always remember you by it. Now let us go back to the hotel."

It was after we had left the ferry boat and I was waving to a taxi that I lost her. It is something I haven't been able to understand even now. Three heavily-built Chinese, in black city suits, jostled me as the taxi moved towards me. One of them bowed and apologised in imperfect English while the other two surrounded me, then the three moved off to a waiting car. When I looked around for Leila she had vanished. It was as if the sidewalk had opened and had swallowed her up.

3

I spent fifteen fruitless minutes walking up and down the vast approach to the Star Ferry without seeing Leila, then with a feeling of uneasiness mixed with irritation I took a taxi back to the hotel.

The old reception clerk was dozing behind his counter.

"Did Leila come back?" I asked him.

He opened one heavy eyelid, stared blankly at me and said, "No speak English." and the eyelid snapped shut.

I went to my room. Leila's door was shut. I turned the handle and the door swung open into darkness. I groped for the light switch and turned it on. I looked into the clean little room: no Leila.

Leaving the door open and the light on, I entered my room, also leaving the door open. I sat on the bed, lit a cigarette and waited.

I waited a little more than an hour. Then because it was more comfortable, I stretched out on the bed. In half an hour, lulled by the heat and the heavy eating, I went to sleep.

I woke, feeling hot, damp and uncomfortable. The early morning sun was filtering through the shutters. I raised my head and looked at my strap watch. The time was twenty minutes to eight. I sat up and stared across the passage into Leila's empty room. A creepy sensation moved icily up my spine. I had a sudden feeling that something bad had happened to her. She hadn't run away from me. I was sure of that. She had been spirited away and I could guess why. Someone had decided she not only knew too much but she had been talking too much.

I considered what to do. I got off the bed, closed my door, shaved and washed as best I could in the cracked basin. I put on a clean shirt, then feeling slightly better than a dead man, I stepped into the passage, locked my door and went to the head of the stairs.

A Chinese boy sat behind the counter: probably the reception clerk's grandson.

"Leila hasn't returned to her room," I said.

He giggled with embarrassment and bowed to me. I could see he hadn't understood one word I had said.

I went down the stairs, waved away an eager rickshaw boy and signalled to a passing taxi. I told the driver to take me to police headquarters.

I was lucky. Chief Inspector MacCarthy was getting out of his car as I arrived. He took me to the police canteen where we were served with strong tea in thick white mugs.

I told him the whole story.

I found his attitude infuriating. This was the first time I had ever done business with a British cop. His calm stolid don't-let's-panic manner made my blood pressure rise.

"But something's happened to her," I said, trying to keep from shouting. "I'm sure of it! One moment she was right with me—the next she had vanished and she hasn't returned to the hotel."

He produced his Dunhill pipe and began to fill it.

"My dear chap," he said, "you don't have to get worked up about it. I've had fifteen years' experience handling these girls. They are here today—gone tomorrow. She probably saw someone she thought had more money than you. It is a well-known dodge with these girls They get what they can out of you—then they disappear."

I drank some of the tea and fought against grinding my teeth.

"This is different. We were going back to the hotel—oh, the hell with it! Someone thinks she's talking. She's been kidnapped."

"Talking about what?"

"I'm trying to solve a murder case," I snarled at him. "She was giving me information."

MacCarthy blew expensive-smelling smoke at me. He smiled the way a parent smiles when his first-born has said something cute. I could see he regarded me as just another American screwball.

"What information could she give you to solve a murder that happened in America?" he asked.

"She told me Herman Jefferson rented a luxury villa at Repulse Bay. She told me he suddenly began to make money three months after he married and because he was making money he left his wife."

He smiled that bright Britannic smile that has even fazzed the Russians.

"My dear chap, you shouldn't pay any attention to what a Chinese prostitute tells you—you really shouldn't."

66

"Yeah. I guess I'm simple. You think she was kidding me and was staying out of her room just to give me an uneasy night?"

He blew smoke at me.

"It's part of a prostitute's job to stay out all night."

"Do you know of any Americans living out at Repulse Bay?"

"I believe there are quite a few."

"Would you know if Jefferson had a place out there?"

"If he had, I would have known, but he hadn't."

"So she was kidding me?"

He smiled his diplomatic smile.

"That of course could be the explanation."

I got to my feet. I knew I was wasting time.

"Thanks for the tea. I'll be seeing you."

"Always glad to help."

I took a taxi back to the hotel. The old reception clerk had taken up his position behind the counter. He bowed to me. I would have liked to have questioned him, but the language barrier was too much of a handicap. If I were going to get anywhere, I would have to find an interpreter. It was then I remembered the English-speaking guide, Wong Hop Ho, who had given me his card at the airport. He might be able to help me.

I went to my room. I saw Leila's door was closed and I paused to knock. There was no answer. I tried the door handle, but the door was locked. I knocked again, listened, hearing nothing, then shrugging, I went to my room.

It was too early to do anything constructive so I took off my jacket, tie and shoes and stretched out on the bed. I did a little thinking that got me nowhere, then I dozed off.

It was after ten o'clock when I woke to the sound of gentle tapping on my door. I swung my legs off the bed and opened the door.

The Chinese boy bobbed, smiling, pointing down the passage. I put on my shoes, then followed him to the reception desk. The old clerk offered me the telephone receiver.

It was Chief Inspector MacCarthy calling me.

"This girl you were telling me about," he said. "You did say you bought her a jade ring last night?"

I stiffened.

"Yes . . . it was imitation jade."

"Would you take a taxi to the Chatham Road police station? It's on the Kowloon side. They have a girl there—could be this girl you're talking about. She is wearing an imitation jade ring."

"Is she dead?" I asked, aware my stomach muscles were tight.

"Oh, very." I could almost smell his expensive tobacco smoke coming over the line. "It'd help if you would identify her. Ask for Sergeant Hamish."

"Another Scotsman?"

"That's right. Lots of Scotsmen in the police force."

"Probably a good thing for Scotland," I said and hung up.

Forty minutes later, I walked up the steps leading to the Chatham Road police station. Just inside the large lobby was a big frame hanging on the wall containing a number of gruesome morgue pictures: photographs of some fifty dead Chinese men and women who had been found in the Straits or in the streets with an appeal both in English and in Chinese to identify them.

The desk sergeant showed me into a tiny office where a hard-faced young man with blond wavy hair and a cop stare was examining a file. He nodded to me when I introduced myself. He said his name was Sergeant Hamish.

"You have a body for me to look at," I said.

He took from his pocket a battered briar pipe. The Hong Kong police seemed to be pipe-smoking types. I watched him fill it as his cold, green eyes considered me without much interest.

"That's right. The Chief Inspector seemed to think you could identify her. She was fished out of the Straits last night around two. Not much of her left. She must have been caught by one of the ferry steamers from the look of her."

I felt sweat sticking my shirt to my back.

He got to his feet.

"These damn people are always killing themselves," he said conversationally. "Every day we collect half a dozen bodies. The Chinese just don't seem to take their lives seriously."

We went down a passage, across a yard and into the morgue. From the number of forms under the coarse twill sheets, business seemed pretty brisk this morning.

He led me to a table, covered with a thick rubber sheet. He lifted a corner of the sheet, groped under it and produced a small amber-coloured hand on which was an imitation jade ring.

"I've had eggs and bacon for breakfast," he said chattily. "If you can identify her by the ring, it'll save me risking a throw-up."

I looked at the ring and the small, slim fingers. It was the ring I had bought Leila.

"That's the ring," I said, and I felt really bad.

He put the hand back out of sight.

"Okay, I'll tell the Chief Inspector."

I reached forward and lifted the rubber sheet. I looked for a long moment at what was left of Leila. I wished I hadn't, but I had to say goodbye to her. I dropped the sheet into place.

I remembered her sighing with happy contentment after we had eaten that memorial meal. I saw again her sturdily-built little back as she had walked ahead of me. I hadn't known her for long, but her personality had impressed me. I felt I had lost someone important.

There was a detective waiting for me on the other side of the ferry. He was a large red-faced man who said his name was Mac-

68

Pherson: there seemed no end to these Scotsmen. He took me back to the hotel in a police jeep.

He talked to the reception clerk in haltering Chinese, then took the key of Leila's room.

As we went down the passage, he said, "The old coot's cagey. We would close up this hole. He isn't admitting she was a tart—can't say I blame him."

I hated him for sentimental reasons. Leila, I felt, deserved something better for an epitaph than being called a tart by a Scotch cop.

MacPherson unlocked her bedroom door and moved into the tiny room. I remained in the passage, looking in. With professional thoroughness, he began to search the room. There were only three dresses hanging in the cupboard and only one set of underwear in one of the drawers. Leila's belongings were pathetically small.

MacPherson gave a sudden grunt as he peered into the bottom of the cupboard.

"I thought as much . . ." he muttered, bent and came up with a small strip of tinfoil. He smoothed the foil out carefully. It appeared to come from a pack of ten cigarettes.

"Know what this is?" he asked, showing me the foil. In its centre was a black smoky smudge.

"You tell me," I said.

He bent once again and peered into the cupboard and this time he came up with a tiny, half-burnt candle: the kind you put on birthday cakes.

He sat on the side of the bed, holding the tinfoil and the candle and became expansive.

"She was a heroin addict," he said. "Something like a dozen drug addicts kill themselves every week."

"What makes you so sure?" I asked.

"Anyone having these two little gadgets is an addict," MacPherson said. "Know how it works? They put heroin in the fold of the foil. They hold the lighted candle under the foil and then sniff up the fumes. It can be done in a few seconds. You know something? The stupidest thing the Government ever did was to wage war on opium smokers. They thought it was the easiest thing in the world to stamp out. Opium smokers have to have a room, a bed and the apparatus for smoking which is not only extensive but expensive. We never have any trouble in finding the room and smashing up the apparatus. An opium pipe costs quite a lot of money, and after a while the smokers got fed up with us breaking up their beds and their pipes and chasing them over the roofs. We kidded ourselves we were putting a stop to the drug traffic, but how wrong we were." He pushed his hat to the back of his head while he looked at me. "The addicts found they could get heroin from opium and all they needed was a piece of tinfoil and a candle. They can inhale this poison anywhere: in the movies, public conveniences, trams, buses, taxis —anywhere. You keep your eyes open and you'll see bits of candle grease in most unexpected places. That'll tell you, as it does us, someone has been inhaling heroin. Opium smoking is an addiction, but it isn't a killer. But make no mistake about it: heroin kills. If we had let the Chinks smoke their opium, we wouldn't be trying hopelessly to cope with heroin addicts."

I rubbed the side of my jaw.

"Thanks for the lecture," I said, "but I don't think she committed suicide and I don't think she was a heroin addict. I think she was murdered and these two little gadgets were planted for you to find."

MacPherson's stolid face showed no change of expression. He produced the inevitable pipe and began to load it.

"Think so?" he asked, an amused note in his voice. "The Chief said you were a private investigator. I've read Chandler and Hammet—they wrote fiction. This happens to be real life."

"So it does," I said. "Well, never mind. I don't suppose it is very important."

"What makes you think she was murdered?" he asked with no show of interest.

"Nothing that would convince you. What are you going to do with her things?"

"I'll take them to the station. Maybe someone will claim them. The old coot doesn't know if she had any relations. I've talked to him before—he never knows anything about anything." He got to his feet. "I wouldn't worry your brains about her." He tossed Leila's belongings into a cheap fibre suitcase he found at the top of the cupboard. "If you had to deal with as many cases as we do like this, you wouldn't give it a second thought."

"I'm sure. That's the idea."

He looked thoughtfully at me.

"What idea?" he asked.

"The men who killed her would want you not to give a second thought, wouldn't they?"

He suddenly grinned.

"Oh, come off it. We handle hundreds of these suicide cases. . . ."

I was sick of him.

"I heard you the first time." I crossed the passage to my room. "I'll be here for a few more days if you should want me."

He peered at me, losing some of his confidence.

"What makes you think I'll want you?" he asked.

"Well, we could read a detective story together," I said and shut the door in his face.

I felt now was the time to spend some of old man Jefferson's money. I was sure the reception clerk could tell me more than he had told MacPherson if there was a cash inducement.

As soon as I was sure MacPherson had left, I went down to where the old clerk was sitting. He eyed me suspiciously but when I made motions to the telephone, he bowed a reluctant permission.

I called Wong Hop Ho's number. He answered immediately as if he had been sitting by the receiver waiting for me to call.

"Remember me?" I said. "You gave me your card at the airport. I need an interpreter."

"It will give me great pleasure, sir," he said.

"Will you meet me outside the Shanghai and Hong Kong Bank in half an hour?"

He said he would be delighted to be there.

"I would like a car."

He said it would be a pleasure to arrange anything for me. He was entirely at my disposal. It didn't sound as if business was over brisk for Mr. Wong Hop Ho.

I thanked him and hung up. Then bowing to the reception clerk who bowed back, I left the hotel and took a taxi to the bank.

I cashed some of the travellers' cheques Janet West had given me and with my hip pocket bulging with Hong Kong dollars, I waited on the sidewalk for Wong Hop Ho to appear.

He arrived ten minutes later, driving a glittering Packard. We shook hands and I told him my name. He said he would be happy if I called him Wong. All his American clients called him that and he would consider it an honour for me to do so too.

I got in the car beside him.

"We'll go back to my hotel," I said. "I want some information from the reception clerk who doesn't speak English." As he looked faintly surprised, I went on, "I am a private investigator and I am working on a case."

He flashed his gold teeth at me in a delighted smile.

"I read many detective stories," he said. "It is a pleasure to meet a real-life detective, sir."

I lugged out some of my dollars and offered him fifty of them.

"Will this take care of your fees for a day or so?" I said. "I'll probably need you from time to time in a hurry."

He said that would be quite satisfactory, but the car would have to be considered as an extra. As I was spending Jefferson's money, I said that would be all right. I was sure I could have bargained with him, but I wanted his full co-operation and I felt I might not get it if I cut corners.

We drove to the hotel and leaving the car on the waterfront, we crossed the road and mounted the stairs to the hotel lobby.

"This is not a good hotel," Wong said on the way up. "I would not advise you to stay here, sir. I can arrange for a nice room for you at a distinguished hotel if that would please you."

"Let's leave it for the moment," I said. "Right now I have a job to do."

We arrived in front of the old reception clerk who bowed to me and looked blankly at Wong who looked blankly back at him.

"Tell him I want to ask some questions," I said to Wong. "I will pay him if he can help me. Wrap it up so he won't take offence."

Wong went off into a long speech in Cantonese with a certain amount of bowing. Half-way through the speech, I got out my roll of money and counted out ten five-dollar bills, made them into a neat little roll and put the rest away.

The old reception clerk immediately took more interest in what I was holding than in what Wong was saying. Finally, Wong said it would be a pleasure for the clerk to answer any of my questions.

I produced the morgue photograph of Jo-An.

"Ask him if he knows this girl."

After staring at the photograph, the reception clerk got in a huddle with Wong who then told me the girl used to live at the hotel. She left fifteen days ago without paying her hotel bill and was I willing to pay it?

I said I wasn't.

After further questions, Wong went on, "She was married to an American gentleman who shared her room here. His name was Herman Jefferson and he died unfortunately in a car accident. It was after this gentleman had died, the girl left without paying her bill."

I produced the photograph of Jefferson that Janet West had given me.

"Ask him if he knows who this is?" I said to Wong.

There was an exchange of words after the clerk had stared glassily at the photograph, then Wong said, "It is the American gentleman who lived here."

"How long did he live here?"

Through Wong, the reception clerk said he had lived in the hotel until he was killed.

This was the first false note in the interview. Leila had said Jefferson had left nine months ago. Now this old buzzard was saying he lived in the hotel up to three weeks ago when he had died.

"I heard Jefferson only stayed here for three months," I said,

72

"then he left his wife and lived elsewhere. That would be some nine months ago."

Wong looked surprised. He talked earnestly to the reception clerk, then he said, puzzled, "He is quite sure the American gentleman remained here until he died."

If the reception clerk was telling the truth, then Leila had been lying.

"Tell him Leila said Jefferson left here nine months ago. Tell him I think he is lying."

Wong got into a long huddle with the reception clerk, then suddenly, smiling, he turned to me. "He is not lying, Mr. Ryan. The girl was mistaken. Jefferson left early in the morning and returned very late. It is easy to see why this girl didn't meet him and imagined he had left."

"Then why did Jo-An tell her he had left?" I demanded.

The reception clerk had no answer to that one. He drew in his neck like a startled tortoise and blinked at me. He began to fidget and I could see he was thinking he had given full value for money and he would be glad to be left in peace.

Wong said, "He does not know the answer to that question, sir."

"What did Jefferson do for a living?" I asked, shifting ground.

The reception clerk said he didn't know.

"Did any Europeans ever come to see him here?"

The answer to that one was no.

"Did Jo-An ever have any friends to visit her?"

The answer again was no.

I realised with a feeling of irritated frustration I was getting nowhere. I had come around in a full circle unless Leila had been telling the truth.

"Did Jo-An leave any of her things in her room when she left?" I asked casually.

This was a trap question and the reception clerk walked into it.

"No," he said through Wong. "She left nothing."

I pounced on him.

"Then how did she manage to walk out of here with her belongings and not pay her bill?" I demanded.

Wong saw the fairness of this and he barked at the old man. For a moment he hesitated, then scowling, he said she had left a suitcase but he was holding it against the rent.

I said I wanted to see it. After some more talk, the old reception clerk got up and led me down the passage to the room next to Leila's. He unlocked the door and produced a cheap imitation leather suitcase from under the bed.

Wong, who had followed us, said, "This case belonged to the girl, sir."

I examined the suitcase. It was locked.

73

"You two wait outside."

When they had gone, I closed and bolted the door. It didn't take me a couple of minutes to force the locks on the suitcase.

Jo-An possessed a slightly better outfit than Leila, but not a great deal better. I turned over the things I found. At the bottom of the suitcase was a large white envelope, its flap tucked. I opened the envelope and shook out a glossy print of Herman Jefferson: a replica of the photograph Janet West had given me. Across the foot of the photograph was scrawled: *For my wife, Jo-An.* I stared at the hard gangster face, then returned the photograph to the envelope and replaced it where I had found it.

I sat on the bed and lit a cigarette. I wondered how Janet West, miles away in Pasadena City, and Jo-An in Hong Kong could both have owned the same photograph. I told myself that Jefferson must have given it to them, but suddenly and far away, a note of interrogation started up in my mind.

I thought back on the conversation I had had with Leila. What the reception clerk had said didn't tally with what she had said . . . one or the other was lying. Why should Leila have lied?

After some more thought I came to the conclusion there was no point in remaining in this sordid little hotel. I would have to look elsewhere to find the clue to this mystery.

I got to my feet, crossed the room and stepped out into the passage.

Wong was leaning up against the wall, smoking a cigarette. He straightened and bowed as I came out. The reception clerk probably had gone back to his desk: he wasn't there.

"I hope everything is satisfactory, sir," he said.

"I guess," I said. "I'm leaving here. Is there a hotel at Repulse Bay?"

He looked faintly surprised.

"Why, yes, sir. There is the Repulse Bay Hotel: a very fine hotel. Would you like me to arrange accommodation for you there?"

"If you can fix it, I'd like to move in right away."

"You realise, sir, the hotel is rather out of the way. If you are thinking of seeing Kowloon, it isn't very convenient."

"That won't worry me. Tell the old guy I'm checking out and get my bill."

"There are no further questions you wish to ask him?" Wong asked, his face showing disappointment.

"No. Let's get out of here."

Thirty minutes later we were in the Packard, driving along the beautiful road towards Repulse Bay.

Repulse Bay turned out to be something very special and the hotel matched it. To my thinking the set-up with its mountains, its concealed bays with an emerald green sea looked better than most of the pleasure spots I'd ever visited, and in my time, I had been lucky to have visited a number of them.

Wong managed to get me a room in the hotel overlooking the bay. He left me the Packard and departed with much bowing, assuring me he was at my service should I need him again.

I got busy as soon as I had unpacked by beginning on the telephone book and then talking to the reception clerk of the hotel probing for a lead to Herman Jefferson. Neither the telephone book nor the clerk had heard of Herman Jefferson.

I then asked the hall porter on the theory a hall porter of a good hotel knows everything. I asked him if he knew who owned a villa close by with steps down to the sea into a small harbour complete with boat.

He regarded me thoughtfully before saying, "You mean Mr. Lin Fan's villa, sir? It is now occupied by Mr. Enright and his sister: they are Americans."

"Did you ever hear if a guy named Herman Jefferson lived there?" I asked.

He shook his head. I could see he was getting a little bored with me.

"Jefferson? No, I don't know the name, sir."

Later in the afternoon, I put on a pair of swim trunks and went down to the crowded beach. I hired a pedallo and took it out into the bay. After some hard, solid work, I got in a position to see the whole coastline. I quickly spotted Lin Fan's villa. It was situated on a promontory, isolated and very lush, with a terrace garden and winding steps leading down to a small harbour where a fast-looking speedboat was moored.

I propelled my boat towards the villa and when I got within two or three hundred yards of the harbour I paused to study the place, thinking if Herman Jefferson had really rented this place as Leila had said he had, then he must have suddenly found the opportunity of making really big money. But had he? Had Jo-An told Leila he had rented this villa to save face? It was the kind of lie one woman might tell another.

I suddenly became aware of two tiny sparkling dots showing from a top window of the villa and I moved on. I had a sudden naked feeling. I propelled my craft along the coast for ten minutes, knowing someone was watching me from the villa through a pair of field glasses, the lenses of which were catching the sun. Then I turned my craft, still aware I was being watched and made my way back to the beach.

I glanced up at the villa as I passed it. The two sparkling dots remained focused on me. I tried to look like a tourist, and I asked myself why I was creating so much interest. I got back to the beach as the sun was going down, and I returned to the hotel, wondering what my next move should be.

I was still undecided the following morning. Around ten o'clock, I went down to the beach. After a quick swim, I stretched myself out on the sand and pushed Herman Jefferson, Janet West, old man Jefferson and poor little Leila out of my mind. I gave myself up to the sun, the sound of the surf and to the feeling of surrender that Hong Kong gives you which is hard to resist.

I lay there for maybe an hour, dozing and letting the sun soak into me. Then I became aware that someone had passed close to me and I lazily opened my eyes.

She was tall and slim and burned a golden brown by the sun. Her salient points which were interesting were scarcely concealed by her scarlet bikini. I saw most men lying on the beach were staring at her . . . so I stared too.

She walked across the hot sand towards the sea, swinging a big sun hat in her hand. Her hair was the colour of ripe corn. She was as intriguing and as beautiful as a motif from a Brahms's symphony.

I watched her drop her hat carelessly on the sand and then slide into the sea. She swam well with strong expert strokes that took her quickly out to the distant raft. I watched her hoist herself onto the raft and she sat with her feet in the water. She looked lonely out there all on her own and I had a sudden urge to keep her company.

I took a running dive into the sea and set out towards the raft with my best racing stroke which is impressive so long as I don't have to keep it up too long.

I broke water a few yards from the raft, and hoisted myself up onto it.

She was lying on her side, her breasts heavy in their slight support, her eyes looking directly into mine.

"Tell me if I'm spoiling a beautiful solitude," I said, "and I'll swim away."

She studied me. Now I was at close quarters, I could see she was a woman who had had plenty of experience with men. She had that air about her. She had inquiring, probing eyes of a woman who is interested in men.

"I was rather hoping for company," she said and smiled. Her voice had that husky sexy tone you sometimes hear, but not often. "Who are you? You've only just arrived, haven't you?"

"My name is Nelson Ryan," I told her. "I was named after

76

the English Admiral. My father spent all his spare time reading English naval history. He was nuts about Nelson."

She rolled over on her back and her hard pointed breasts thrust towards the sky.

"I'm Stella Enright," she said. "I live here. It's nice to meet a new face. Are you staying long?"

Just how lucky can a man be? I wondered. Here is the sister of the man who rents Lin Fan's villa. Then I recalled the sparkling dots of the watching field glasses. Maybe it wasn't luck. Maybe this meeting was a little more subtle than luck.

"I wish I was . . . a week perhaps." I took from my waterproof pocket a pack of cigarettes and a lighter. "You're lucky to be able to live here. This place is pretty nice."

I offered her a cigarette and we lit up.

"It's all right . . . now is the best season, but the summer is bad." She blew a thin cloud of smoke into the still air. "My brother is writing a book on Hong Kong. I run the house." She lifted her head to look at me. "Are you staying at the hotel?"

"Yes. You have a house?"

"We have rented a villa. It belongs to a Chinese gambler."

"Lin Fan?"

Her eyes showed surprise.

"That's right. How would you know?"

"I heard." I hesitated, then decided to push it as far as it would go. "I thought Herman Jefferson rented that place."

She lifted golden eyebrows in what seemed to me genuine astonishment.

"Herman Jefferson? Do you know him?"

"He happens to come from my home town. Do you?"

"He's dead . . . killed in a car accident."

"I heard that. Did you know him?"

"Harry—that's my brother—knew him. I met him once or twice. So you know him? Harry will be interested. It was an awful thing the way he died . . . awful for his Chinese wife."

"You knew her?"

"I wouldn't say that. I've seen her . . . a lovely little thing." She flicked ash off her cigarette. "Some Chinese women are really attractive. She was. I could understand Herman falling for her. She was very intriguing." She said it the way most women talk about a woman who is attractive to men: a bitter-sweet touch I didn't miss. "She took his body back to America. I suppose she will stay there. After all, Herman's father is a millionaire. I guess he'll look after her."

I resisted the temptation to tell her Jo-An was dead.

"Someone told me Herman came into money, left her and rented your villa."

She half sat up, frowning.

"What an extraordinary story! Who told you that?"

77

"Oh, someone," I said casually. "It isn't true?"

"Why no . . . of course not!" She suddenly relaxed, smiling at me. "It's too ridiculous. Herman was. . . ." She paused, then shrugged her naked shoulders. "Well, frankly, Herman was a no-gooder. I didn't like him very much, but he amused Harry. He just wasn't any good. He went native. He never had any money. There were rumours he lived on this Chinese girl. He could never have afforded to rent Lin Fan's villa. The very idea is ridiculous. Whoever told you that?"

The sound of a fast-moving motor-boat made both of us look out to sea. Coming towards us was a speedboat, cleaving through the sea and throwing up a white spray.

"Here's Harry now," Stella said and rising to her feet, balancing herself on the rocking raft, she waved.

The boat slowed and then the engines cut. It drifted close to the raft. A tall, sun-burned man, wearing a blue and white sweat shirt and white shorts grinned amiably at Stella. His handsome face was a trifle fleshy from good living and there was a network of fine veins, well disguised by his heavy tan that told me he liked the extra drink.

"I thought I'd pick you up. It's lunch-time." He looked inquiringly at me. "Who's your boy friend?"

"This is Nelson Ryan. He knew Herman Jefferson," Stella said and looked at me. "This is my brother, Harry."

We nodded to each other.

"You knew Herman?" Harry said. "Well, what do you know? You here for some time?"

"Not more than a week, worse luck," I said.

"Look, if you have nothing better to do tonight, why not come over to our place and have dinner with us? I'll pick you up in the boat . . . it's the only way to get to the place. Will you do that?"

"Why, sure I'd be glad to, but I don't want to trouble you to pick me up."

"That's nothing. Be down on the beach at eight o'clock. I'll be there, and after dinner we'll take the boat out. It's wonderful at night in this tub." He looked at Stella. "Are you coming?"

"Take me back to the beach first. I've left my hat." She climbed into the boat. I couldn't take my eyes off her slim, sun-tanned back as she got into the boat. She looked suddenly over her shoulder, catching me staring and she smiled as if she knew what was going on in my mind. "I'll see you tonight," she said, and with a wave of her hand she settled herself beside her brother. He nodded to me and the boat roared away across the bay towards the beach.

I lit a cigarette and dangled my feet in the water, my mind busy. I sat there for the next half hour, my body soaking in the sun, then feeling hungry, I slid into the water and swam to the shore.

I was down on the beach at eight o'clock, and after a few minutes' wait, I saw the speedboat come out of the darkness. The driver was a powerfully-built Chinese who assisted me on board as if I were a cripple with abrupt little bows and a steely grip on my arm. Mr. Enright, he explained in guttural English, had been unable to come, and he presented his excuses.

The boat was fast, and within five minues, we arrived at the little harbour below Lin Fan's villa.

I toiled up the steps and reached the terrace, slightly breathless.

Stella, wearing a white evening dress, cut low enough to reveal the tops of her breasts, was lying on a bamboo lounging chair, a highball in her hand, a cigarette between her lips. A young Chinese servant stood expectantly in the shadows. There was no sign of Harry Enright.

"There you are . . ." Stella said, waving the highball at me. "What will you drink?"

I said Scotch and soda and the Chinese servant quickly produced the drink.

"Harry will be here in a moment. Sit there where I can see you."

I could see into the big lounge that led off the terrace. The room was richly furnished in Chinese style with heavy lacquer cabinets, red silk on the walls and a big black mother-of-pearl inlaid table set for dinner.

"Some place you have here," I said.

"Yes . . . it's nice. We were lucky to have got it. We've only been here a few weeks . . . before we had an apartment in Kowloon. We like this much better."

"Who was here before you?" I asked.

"I don't think anyone was. The owner only decided to let the villa recently. He's now living in Macau."

Just then Harry Enright came out onto the terrace. He shook hands with me and then sat down opposite me.

The Chinese servant made him a highball.

After the usual polite chit-chat about the view and the villa, he asked, "Are you here on a business trip?"

"I'm on vacation," I said. "I had the chance for a week or so off and couldn't resist coming here."

"Don't blame you." He studied me in a friendly way. "I'm crazy about Hong Kong. Stella was telling me you come from Pasadena City. Did you know Herman Jefferson well?"

"I know his father better. The old man is worried about Herman. He asked me to make inquiries about him when he heard I was coming this way."

Enright looked interested.

"Is that right? What sort of inquiries?"

"Well, Herman had been out here for five years. He seldom wrote home. His father has no idea what he did with himself. He was pretty shaken when Herman wrote he had married an Asian."

Enright nodded and looked over at Stella.

"I bet he was."

"I think the old boy feels bad that he didn't do more for his son while he was alive. Have you any idea what Herman did for a living?"

"I don't think he did anything," Enright said slowly. "He was a bit of a mystery. Personally, I liked him, but he wasn't anyone's choice." He grinned at Stella. "She couldn't stand the sight of him for one."

Stella moved impatiently.

"Don't exaggerate," she said. "I admit I didn't take to him. He thought any woman had to fall for him . . . I don't like that type."

Enright laughed.

"Well, you didn't fall for him," he said, and I caught a jeering note in his voice. "Probably sour grapes. Well, I liked him."

"But then you are amoral," his sister said. "You like anyone who will amuse you."

The conversation was interrupted by the Chinese servant announcing dinner was ready. We moved into the lounge.

It was a Chinese meal which I enjoyed. We talked about this and that. Enright was very gay but I noticed Stella seemed preoccupied as if she were only half listening to our conversation.

As the meal was finishing, she asked abruptly, "Who told you Herman rented this villa, Mr. Ryan?"

"Herman rented this villa?" Enright cut in. "For Pete's sake! Did someone tell you that?" He looked quizzingly at me.

"A Chinese girl," I said. "I met her at the Celestial Empire Hotel where Jefferson lived. She told me."

"I wonder why?" Stella said, frowning. "What an absurd thing to say."

I lifted my shoulders.

"She was probably kidding me," I said. For the past ten or twenty seconds I had suddenly felt I was being watched. I glanced around the room. "I asked her for information about Herman. Maybe she felt she should tell me something to earn what I was offering her." There was a big mirror opposite me. I looked into it. Behind me, in the lobby outside the lounge reflected in the mirror, I could see a squat shadowy figure of a man. He was Chinese, wearing a European suit. He was studying me intently. For a brief second our eyes met in the reflection of the mirror, then he moved back into the darkness of the lobby and disappeared. I felt a prickle run up my spine. There was something sinister and menacing about the man and I had trouble not to show by my expression I had seen him watching me.

"Chinese will say anything if they imagine it is what you want them to say," Enright said. I was aware he was looking intently at me. "Chinese girls are the most fluent liars in the world."

"Is that a fact?" I said. I looked again into the mirror, then with an effort shifted my eyes back to Enright. "Well. . . ."

"Let's go on the terrace," Stella said, getting to her feet. "Will you have a brandy?"

I said no, and we wandered out onto the terrace. The moon had come up and was reflecting on the sea.

"I've a couple of telephone calls to make," Enright said. "If you'll excuse me, then we might take the boat out. Would you like that?"

I looked at Stella.

"If you like it, it suits me fine."

"Oh, I'll like it," she said in a resigned voice. "Harry can't think of anything except his blessed boat."

By then Enright had gone. She slid her arm through mine and led me to the balustrade. We stood looking at the sea.

"In a way that Chinese girl is lucky," Stella said, and I caught a wistful note in her voice. "I expect Herman's father will provide for her. I hear he is very rich."

"She lost her husband," I said, still not sure if I should tell her that Jo-An was dead.

She made an impatient movement.

"It was good riddance. Now she is free with money and she is in America." She heaved a sigh. "I wish I were back in New York."

"Is that where you come from?"

"Hmm . . . I haven't been back for over a year now. I'm homesick."

"Can't you go? Do you have to stay here?"

She started to say something then stopped. After a long pause, she said, "I don't have to stay here, of course, but my brother and I have done things together for so long it's become a habit."

She pointed to the mountain ahead of us. "Doesn't that look lovely in the moonlight?"

I guessed she was deliberately changing the subject and I wondered why, but I played along. We were still admiring the view when Enright came onto the terrace.

"Well, let's go," he said. "How would you like to see Aberdeen—it's the fishermen's village here? It's quite something to see."

"Why, sure," I said, and we left the terrace and filed down the steps to the boat. Stella and I sat immediately behind Enright who took the driver's wheel. He sent the boat roaring out to sea.

It wasn't possible to talk against the sound of the powerful engines. Stella sat away from me, staring out into the moonlit night. There was a depressed expression on her face as if she were concentrating on something that saddened her. My mind was busy too, turning over the bits of information I had gathered. I still couldn't believe that Leila had lied to me. Either

81

the Enrights were misinformed or they too, like the reception clerk at the Celestial Empire Hotel, were lying about Herman Jefferson . . . but why?

The village of Aberdeen was one of the most fantastic sights I have seen. The harbour was crammed with junks, shoulder to shoulder and swarming with Chinese with their relations and children. There was no hope of entering the harbour so Enright dropped anchor and we took a sampan rowed by a thirteen-year-old Chinese girl to the landing-stage. We spent an hour wandering around the tiny, interesting bay village, then Stella said she was tired and we returned to the boat. As we were being rowed in the sampan to the boat, Stella said, "Have you been to the islands yet? You should see them. You can take a ferry."

"Not yet . . . no."

"If you have nothing better to do tomorrow, I'm going to Silver Mine Bay. We could go together. I have a visit to make. While I'm visiting you might like to look at the waterfall. It is something to see, then we could come back together."

"I'd like it fine," I said.

"My sister is a very charitable soul," Enright said. "We had a servant when we first came here. She was very old and we had to get rid of her. She lives at Silver Mine Bay. Stella visits her from time to time. She takes her things."

He started the motor-boat engine and that stopped all talking. It took us twenty minutes or so to reach the villa. Stella left the boat and Enright said he would run me back to the hotel.

"Good night," Stella said, pausing at the bottom of the steps to smile at me. "The ferry-boat leaves at two. I'll look out for you on the pier."

I thanked her for a wonderful evening and she lifted her hand in a little wave and then started up the steps as Enright opened the throttle and sent the boat roaring in the direction of the hotel.

He dropped me at the landing-stage.

"When did you say you were leaving?" he asked as I climbed out of the boat.

"About a week's time . . . I'm not sure."

"Well, you must come again. It's been nice meeting you."

We shook hands and then I watched him drive the boat out to sea.

I walked slowly up the beach towards the hotel. I couldn't get out of my mind the sinister squat figure of the Chinese I had seen reflected in the mirror. I had an instinctive feeling he meant trouble.

The following morning I found myself in the office of the Third Secretary, American Consul.

I had had a little trouble getting to him, but by bearing down on old man Jefferson's name, I was finally and reluctantly admitted to his office.

He was a fat, smooth-looking bird, surrounded by an atmosphere of diplomatic immunity. He read my card which lay on his desk by peering gingerly at it as if he felt by touching it he might pick up an incurable disease.

"Nelson Ryan . . . private investigator," he intoned and then sat back and lifted supercilious eyebrows. "What can I do for you?"

"I'm working for J. Wilbur Jefferson," I said. "I'm making inquiries about his son, Herman Jefferson, who died here in a road accident about seventeen days ago."

He fed a cigarette into his fat face.

"So?"

"He was a resident of Hong Kong. I take it he would have had to register here."

"That is correct."

"Can you tell me his last address?"

He moistened one fat finger and smoothed down his left eyebrow.

"Well, I suppose I could give it to you, but is it necessary? It's a dead file now. It may take a little time to get it from the vaults."

"Is that what you want me to tell Mr. Jefferson?" I asked. "I can't imagine he would toss his bonnet over a windmill to hear a Third Secretary of the American Consul couldn't be bothered to help him."

He looked suddenly wary. Probably he had suddenly remembered just how much water the old man could draw if he wanted to.

Slightly flustered, he picked up the telephone and said, "Oh, Miss Davenport, will you bring me Herman Jefferson's file . . . yes, Herman Jefferson. Thank you." He replaced the receiver and hoisted a weary smile on his fat face, showing me his set of porcelain choppers. "Yeah . . . J. Wilbur Jefferson. I remember now . . . the millionaire. How is the old gentleman?"

"Still ready and willing to kick a backside when it needs kicking," I said cheerfully. "He has a hell of a long leg and a hell of a heavy boot."

The Third Secretary, whose name was Harris Wilcox, winced, then laughed as convincingly as a newly-wed husband laughs when meeting his mother-in-law for the first time.

"Wonderful how these old tycoons last," he said. "He'll probably see us both into the ground."

There was a pause while we sat staring at each other for about two minutes, then the door opened and Miss Davenport, a willowy girl of around twenty-five, moved her well-built body to the desk and put a file, slim enough to be empty, before Mr. Wilcox. She glanced at me, then went out waving her hips the way secretaries with hips do while we both watched her until the door closed, then Wilcox opened the file.

"All his papers went back with the body," he said apologetically, "but we should have something here." He peered at the single sheet of paper in the file, then shook his head. "Not a great deal, I'm afraid. His last address was the Celestial Empire Hotel. He arrived in Hong Kong on September 3rd, 1956, and he has lived at the hotel ever since. He married a Chinese girl last year."

"What did he do for a living?"

Wilcox again peered at the sheet of paper.

"He's down here as an exporter, but I understand he didn't do anything for a living. I guess he had private means although I understand that he lived very rough."

"Would it surprise you to know he rented a luxury villa at Repulse Bay?" I asked.

Wilcox stared blankly at me.

"He did? He should have registered a change of address if he had done so. Are you sure? What villa?"

"The villa belonging to Lin Fan."

"Oh, no, Mr. Ryan, I know that villa. Jefferson couldn't possibly have afforded such a place. It would cost in English money at least four hundred pounds a month."

"Right now the villa is rented by Harry Enright who lives there with his sister," I said.

Wilcox nodded. His face showed sudden animation.

"That's right. Enright took the villa over from some Englishman. I forget his name. Nice guy . . . I mean Enright, and what a sister!" He leered. "Probably the most attractive woman in Hong Kong."

"I understood the villa was empty before Enright took it."

"Oh no. There was some Englishman there. I never met him."

"Jefferson and this Chinese girl were really married?"

He stared at me.

"Of course. They were married here. I could show you a copy of the marriage certificate if you want to see it."

"Yeah: I'd like to see it."

He did some telephoning, then as we waited, he said, "I remember her well—a pretty little thing. I had the job of clearing her papers and despatching the coffin . . . a sad affair." He tried to look sad. "I was sorry for her."

Miss Davenport minced in, gave Wilcox the certificate and

84

then duck-tailed out. When we had got through watching her exit, Wilcox passed the certificate across the desk to me. I examined it. It did prove that Jefferson had married Jo-An a year ago. I learned that Frank Belling and Mu Hai Ton had been witnesses of the ceremony.

"Who is Frank Belling?" I asked, showing Wilcox the certificate.

He shook his head.

"I've no idea. A friend of Jefferson's I guess. He must be English. We've no record of him."

"And the girl?"

"I wouldn't know. Probably a friend of Mrs. Jefferson." He tapped his porcelain teeth gently with the end of his fountain pen and looked sideways at his desk clock.

I decided there was nothing further to learn from him so I got to my feet.

"Well, thanks," I said. "I mustn't take up your time."

He said it was a pleasure to have met me. I could see it gave him more pleasure to see me go.

"You never met Herman Jefferson?" I asked at the door.

"Funnily enough I didn't. He kept to the Chinese quarter. He seemed never to mix with my friends."

I left the building and walked slowly over to where I had parked the Packard. On my way I had to sidestep two uniformed Chinese policemen who were dragging along a beggar woman and a screaming child. No one seemed to pay any attention to this little scene. When you have an influx of a hundred thousand refugees illegally entering this small island every year, such a sight probably becomes commonplace, but it depressed me.

I sat in the car and turned over in my mind what I had learned. Not much, but perhaps I had a small lead to work on. I decided I wanted to talk to this Chinese girl, Mu Hai Ton, and also to Frank Belling.

I drove to the Central Police Station and asked to speak to Chief Inspector MacCarthy. After a little delay, I was shown into his office.

The Chief Inspector was cleaning his pipe. He waved me to a chair, blew through his pipe and then began to fill it.

"And what can I do for you this morning?" he asked.

"I'm looking for a man. His name is Frank Belling," I said. "Can you give me a lead on him?"

MacCarthy lit his pipe and puffed smoke towards me. He would have made a poor poker player. Although his face remained expressionless, I saw his eyes become alert and hard.

"Frank Belling?" He removed his pipe and rubbed the warm bowl against the side of his nose. "Why are you interested in him?"

"I don't know that I am. He happened to be a witness at Herman Jefferson's wedding. Do you know him?"

MacCarthy stared blankly at the wall behind me, then reluctantly he nodded.

"Yes . . . we know him," he said. "So he was a witness to Jefferson's wedding. Hmm . . . interesting. You wouldn't know where he is?"

"I'm asking you that . . . remember?"

"So you are." He leaned forward and straightened his snowy white blotter. "Belling is a man we are anxious to contact. He is a member of a very active drug-running organisation here. We were about ready to grab him when he vanished. We're still trying to find him. It's my bet he's either skipped to Macau or Canton."

"Have you looked for him there?"

"We've made inquiries in Macau, but we haven't any facilities to check on a man in Canton."

I eased myself in the hard upright chair.

"He's English?"

"Yes . . . he's English." MacCarthy tapped down the rising tobacco into the bowl of his pipe. "We know for certain he is part of an organisation here that is causing us a lot of trouble. Large quantities of heroin are being smuggled in from Canton. Up to a couple of weeks ago, Belling was playing an active part in getting the stuff into Hong Kong. We had been watching him for some time, waiting for a big consignment to come in." He relit his pipe, then went on, "We had a tip from one of our informers that delivery was to be made on the first of this month. Then Belling vanished. It's my guess he was tipped off we were ready to grab him and he skipped either to Macau or Canton."

"The first of this month . . . that would be two days before Jefferson died?"

"So it would," MacCarthy said, stared, then asked politely, "Does that mean anything?"

"I'm just getting the facts straight in my mind. The woman witness at the marriage was Chinese: Mu Hai Ton. That name mean anything to you?"

"No."

I lit a cigarette while the Chief Inspector watched with disapproval.

"Do you think Jefferson was hooked up with the drug ring?"

"Maybe," MacCarthy said, shrugging his shoulders. "We never got a iine on him. I've no reason to think so, but if he was friendly with Belling, he could have been."

"You can't give me a line on the girl?"

"I'll check our records. If I get anything I'll let you know." He stared quizzically at me. "You've moved to the Repulse Bay Hotel?"

"That's right."

He shook his head enviously.

"You investigators have a nice life. Everything on the expense account I suppose?"

I grinned at him and got to my feet.

"That's right," I said. "Well, so long and thanks. I'll be seeing you."

I went down into the crowded Queen's Road Central. The time was now half past eleven. I got in the Packard and drove to Wanchai waterfront. Leaving the car, I went into the bar where I had met the Madame who had drunk a glass of milk with me.

The place was empty of customers. Two Chinese waiters talked together behind the bar. They recognised me and one came over, showing gold-capped teeth in a wide smile of welcome.

"Good morning, sir. Very happy to see you again. A drink or perhaps lunch?"

"I'll have a Coke and rum," I said. "Madame around?"

He looked at the clock over the bar.

"She'll be here any moment, sir."

I sat down and toyed with my drink. The Chinese woman didn't appear for half an hour, but to the Chinese that was no time at all. I waved to her as she came in and she crossed the bar to shake hands. She sat down opposite me.

"I am very happy to see you again," she said. "I hope all was satisfactory with the girl."

I grinned at her.

"You pulled a fast one that time. She wasn't Jo-An and you know it."

One of the waiters came over with a pint glass of milk which he set before her. Then he went away.

"That was a mistake," she said. "The girl was more pleasing than Jo-An. I thought you would not mind."

"There is another girl I want to meet," I said. "Her name is Mu Hai Ton. Do you know her?"

Her face was expressionless as she nodded.

"She is one of my very best girls. You will like her very much."

"Only this time," I said, "she will have to prove who she is. I have business to discuss with her."

Madame thought for a moment.

"She will be able to prove who she is. What business do you want to discuss with her?"

"That need not concern you. When can I meet her?"

"I will try to arrange something. When would you like to meet her? Now?"

"Not right now. How about tonight? I'll be here at eight o'clock. Will you arrange for her to be here?"

She nodded.

"If she is the right girl, and if she is co-operative, I will give you fifty dollars."

"She will be the right girl and she will be co-operative," Madame said, a sudden steely expression in her eyes.

I finished my drink.

"Then tonight at eight." I got to my feet. "I will know if she isn't the right girl so don't pull another fast one."

She smiled at me.

"You will be satisfied."

I drove back to the Repulse Bay Hotel, feeling my morning hadn't been wasted.

CHAPTER THREE

1

I LEANED on the rail of the first-class deck of the ferry-boat and watched the third-class passengers fight their way up the gang-plank onto the lower deck.

It was a colourful and interesting sight. Everyone, and they were all Chinese, acted as if the boat was about to sail immediately whereas it had at least a quarter of an hour before pulling away from the Star Ferry pier. Coolies, staggering under enormous burdens slung on bamboo poles, rushed up the gangplank, jostling and pushing as if their lives depended on getting onto the already overcrowded deck. Chinese women, babies strapped on their backs, surrounded by sharp-eyed children in padded coats, pushed and shoved their way along the pier. Two slim Chinese girls in black coats and trousers came up the gangplank at a trot carrying between them on a bamboo pole a large sausage-shaped wicker basket in which lay a full-grown and grunting pig. A half-naked Chinese youth, his right shoulder horribly deformed through carrying heavy burdens slung on his carrying pole, grinned happily as he bustled a group of tiny children ahead of him. Two smart uniformed Chinese policemen stood, their thumbs hooked in their revolver belts and watched the scene with a fatherly tolerance.

I shifted my gaze to look at the few first-class passengers who were coming aboard. There was no sign of Stella, but I was sure she would arrive at the last moment. She was the type who timed her entrance. She would never be either too early or too late.

A squat, heavily-built Chinese, wearing a black city suit, a bulky briefcase under his arm came up the first-class gang-plank. Looking down at this powerful-built man, I had the image of a figure reflected in the mirror at Enright's hired villa. I was suddenly sure that this was the man I had seen watching me from the darkened lobby.

I watched him come, studying him. He could be any age up to forty, but there was great strength and power in his squat limbs and he moved with the speed and ease of a gymnast.

I told myself all Chinese look alike and I was being cock-eyed to think this was the man who had been watching me in Enright's villa, but the feeling persisted even when he walked past me without looking at me and sat down, opening a newspaper with a flick of his wrists and hiding himself behind it.

At one minute to sailing time, I saw Stella, wearing an apple-green cotton dress and carrying a straw basket, come along the pier. She paused at the foot of the gangplank and waved to me. She was the last passenger to arrive.

I went down the gangplank to take the basket from her to the irritation of two Chinese sailors who were about to wheel the gangplank away.

"Hello," Stella said. "Well, here I am . . . as usual I just made it."

We regained the deck and the ferry moved away from the pier. We sat on the bench seat and talked. The conversation was impersonal and Jefferson wasn't mentioned. As we came in sight of Lantao Island, Stella asked casually what I had been doing all the morning. I told her I had been exploring the back streets of Hong Kong.

"Well, here we are," she said as the boat nosed up to Silver Mine pier. "I've got to leave these things." She waved to the basket. "I'll have to talk to the old dear. I'll be about an hour and a half. Why don't you walk to the waterfall? It's really worth seeing."

"I'll do that. Shall we meet here?"

"The next ferry back is just before six. I'll be here."

She let me carry the basket down to the pier, then she directed me the way to go.

"You follow the path around Butterfly Hill," she said, "then you will come to a bridge. Keep on and you will come to another bridge. Beyond the second bridge is the waterfall." She smiled at me. "It's one of the most attractive sights here."

"I'll find it," I said.

I watched her walk away to a row of poor looking houses festooned with gaily coloured washing. She moved gracefully, avoiding the jog trotting Chinese peasants and the well-fed, cheerful-looking children who swarmed around the skirts of her green dress.

I looked around for the squat Chinese, but he had vanished. I had seen him get off the boat, but now I had no idea where he had got to.

89

I had nothing to do until eight o'clock and I felt ready for a walk. It was a warm sunny day and I was in no hurry. I strolled along the path pointed out to me by Stella and after ten minutes or so, I left the waterfront behind and found myself walking along a deserted footway. After I had passed through a village I later learned was Chung Hau, I was suddenly alone with Butterfly Hill on my right and an expanse of open country to my left.

I reached the waterfall without meeting anyone, duly admired it, and then decided to retrace my steps. It was then that it happened. Something that could have been a large sized hornet zipped past my face. It was followed by the distant sound of a rifle shot.

I spread myself flat on the ground with the reflex action I had had drummed into me during my service in the infantry. As I rolled off the road, there came another rifle shot and the dust was kicked up about two yards from me.

I rolled into the thick grass on the side of the path as yet another rifle shot cracked in the still air. This time he nearly nailed me. The bullet zipped past my head alarmingly close.

Sweating, my heart thumping, I kept moving, rolling over, trying to dig myself into the hard ground. I finally came up against a large rock, and with speed, close to panic, I slid around it and lay flat and waited.

Nothing happened and I began to calm down a little. Whoever was shooting at me was up on the hill. He was probably using a telescopic sight. From the sound of the rifle shot, he was a good quarter of a mile away.

I cursed myself for not bringing my .38, but I was wearing a short sleeved shirt and a pair of slacks: no outfit for carrying a gun. He knew where I was. All he had to do was to wait for me to show. Very cautiously, I lifted my head to look behind me to plan an escape route. A rifle cracked and a bullet flicked past my face. I flatttened out.

There were two of them! The last shot had come immediately behind me. The sniper was closer than the other one . . . too damn close!

They must know by the clothes I was wearing I wasn't armed. There was nothing to stop them now they knew they had missed me with their opening shots to come down and make sure they didn't miss.

I looked at my strap watch. The time was twenty minutes past five. Would Stella come to meet me when I didn't show at the pier? Suppose she walked into these two? Would they kill her as they were trying to kill me?

I started a slow crawl away from the rock. My combat training was still alive in my mind. I slid through the long grass, snake-like, moving downhill. After five minutes of careful manoeuvring,

I was a hundred feet from where I had been. Then, inch by inch, I lifted my head to try to see where I was.

The hiss of the bullet by my face and then the crack of the rifle made me flatten into the ground. These two were either smarter than I thought they were or I was a lot less good as an infantry man.

I slowly shifted my position. It was as well that I did. Another shot cracked the silence and a bullet zunked into the earth just where I had been lying. I told myself it was a lucky shot. The guy had fired at where he imagined I was, but it was far too close for comfort.

I moved farther to my right, then I saw the long grass ceased to exist. Another four feet ahead of me would bring me to barren rocky ground which dipped sharply to a slope, probably to the side of the hill, running down into a valley.

I lay listening and waiting. I heard nothing. Without raising my head, I could see nothing.

I did the Indian trick of putting my ear down on the ground and listening intently. For several minutes I still heard nothing, then I heard him. I guessed he was about fifty yards to my right. He was crawling towards me, hidden in the long grass and he would be on me pretty soon if I didn't do something about it.

I tried to judge just where he was, but that wasn't possible. At least I knew from which direction he was coming. I waited a minute longer, then feeling naked and pretty scared, I rose out of the grass with a quick jinking movement, jumping first right, then left to throw the other joker's aim off. I was aware of a distant crack of a rifle shot. The bullet went wide by yards. I saw a movement in the grass six yards from me and I started for it.

A Chinese, wearing a blue coat and trousers with a baggy black cap rose out of the grass and grinned at me. He was small, thin and wiry. The sun flashed on the knife he held in his hand. I didn't give him a chance to get set. I dived for him, my right hand groping for the knife hand, my left hand for his throat.

I hit him in the chest with my shoulder and we went down into the high grass with a bone shaking impact. I had his wrist and him by the throat. He tried to get his fingers into my eyes, but I slammed the top of my head into his face. I heard him grunt. He didn't stand a chance. He was half my weight and half my strength. I got the knife away from him, then I fastened both hands around his throat. He squirmed under me, but not for long. I squeezed into his skinny throat until I saw his eyes roll up and felt him go limp. Panting a little, I heaved myself off him, keeping flat, wondering if the other joker was on his way down.

I waited some minutes until the Chinese began to move. I crawled around him and sat him up by shoving against his shoulder blades, but keeping flat myself. His cap had fallen off in the struggle. From where the sniper lay my man could have been me and that's what the sniper thought or maybe he didn't care. A rifle cracked and suddenly my man's face was a mask of blood. It was good shooting. I let the limp body drop back into the grass, then I crawled backwards until I was about fifteen yards from the body.

I waited. From time to time I pressed my ear to the ground. It was a long wait. The hands of my watch showed half past six before the sniper lost patience and decided to come down and find out what had happened.

He came with plenty of confidence, knowing I was either dead or harmless. By parting the grass a little I was able to see the hillside from where the last shot had come. I caught sight of him coming down the hill, a rifle under his arm, squat, powerfully built, incongruous in his black city suit . . . the man who had been watching me in the Enright villa and who I had seen on the ferry-boat.

Watching him come, I had a creepy sensation. It had been Stella's idea for me to come to this lonely island. I had been invited to the Enright villa, and this squat Chinese, walking so confidently towards me, had been there to take a look at me. It seemed to me as I lay in the long grass that I had walked into a prepared trap from which I wasn't supposed to escape.

At the rate he was moving, he would be with me in less than ten minutes. I crawled through the grass to collect the long-bladed knife. It didn't give me a lot of confidence. A knife against a rifle isn't fair odds. I looked around and found a flat, heavy stone larger than my hand. I collected that too.

By now the squat Chinese was walking along the path. He had slowed his pace and was moving more cautiously, but he still seemed to have plenty of confidence because he carried the rifle under his arm.

By now I had squirmed farther from the body . . . twenty yards of high grass separated us. The squat Chinese would come on the body before he came on me.

He was now too close for me to watch him. I lay flat, gripping the stone in my right hand and the knife in my left.

I could hear him. I heard him give a little grunt. Cautiously I lifted my head. He had found his pal and was standing over him, staring. He jerked his head up and we looked at each other. The rifle slid from under his arm into his hands. As I threw the stone, he squeezed the trigger. The flying stone spoilt his aim but it wasn't all that bad a shot. The bullet scraped the top of my shoulder. My stone was luckier. The edge of the stone caught his right hand, splitting the skin. He dropped the rifle, and as he bent to pick it up, I was on him.

It was like charging against the side of a house. He had twisted sideways, his legs spread to take the shock of my charge. His hand flashed up and grabbed my wrist. He had fingers like steel. I went flying over his head to land on the ground with a jar that shook the breath out of my body. I was dimly aware I had lost the knife. I was also aware that my fall had brought me to the side of the hill. Letting myself go limp, I started to roll. I heard him coming after me. After I had rolled fifty yards or so, I dug my heels into the soft ground and stopped. I was dizzy and breathless. I saw him coming, a vicious grin on his fat, yellow face, but without the gun.

I was on my feet as he reached me, below him and at a disadvantage, but he was coming too fast to stop. I swerved aside at the moment of impact. He tried to grab me, but his hooked fingers slid off my arm as he went careering past. I swung around and planted my shoe in his fat behind. He pitched forward and slid down the hill on his face.

I found another flat, heavy stone which I snatched up and threw after him. The stone caught him on the back of his head and blood flew. He went on down the hill, kicking up the dust, but limp. Maybe I had smashed his skull. I didn't care. All I knew he wouldn't worry me for some time . . . if ever.

Breathing heavily, feeling a burning in my shoulder, I set off down the path, walking unsteadily, towards the Silver Mine Pier.

2

I walked into the bar on the Wanchai waterfront at exactly eight o'clock. I had showered and changed and had put an adhesive plaster on the bullet graze on my shoulder. It felt sore and hot, but I was lucky it was no worse.

The bar was full. There were about twenty American sailors drinking and dancing and some thirty Chinese girls, all wearing Cheongsams, crowding around the bar or dancing. There were a few Chinese businessmen in the booths, drinking whisky and talking earnestly.

The juke-box was blaring jazz loud enough to break a sensitive eardrum. I stood just inside the door, looking around. The Chinese Madame came out of the noise and the cigarette smoke, smiling. She led me to one of the few vacant booths and sat me down.

"What will you drink?" she asked, standing over me, her hard glittering eyes avoiding my stare.

"A Scotch . . . and you?"

"I'll get you a Scotch."

She went away and I lost sight of her behind the screen of dancers. After a five-minute wait, a waiter come to my table and put down a Scotch and soda. I waited. It was another ten minutes before the Chinese woman came back to my table and sat down. She looked a little worried.

"Mu Hai Ton will see you," she said, "but not here. She wants you to go to her apartment."

Another trap? I wondered. I was still a little shaky after my experience of the afternoon. I was now wearing a suit and had my .38 police special in its holster out of sight but ready for business.

"Where is she?"

"It is not far. I can arrange a taxi for you."

I hesitated, then nodded.

"Okay . . . but how do I know she is the right girl?"

"She has her papers. She will show them to you. She is the right girl."

"Do I go now?"

"She is waiting."

I finished my drink and got to my feet.

"After I've talked to her and after I am satisfied she is the right girl I will pay you fifty Hong Kong dollars."

She smiled stiffly.

"That's all right. I will get you a taxi."

I waited. After a few minutes she returned.

"He knows where to take you. The apartment is on the top floor. You will have no difficulty in finding it."

I said I would be seeing her and I went out into the hot night. The taxi-driver grinned cheerfully at me as I opened the cab door. I got in and he drove off. It was a six-minute drive through the crowded back streets of the Chinese quarter. The taxi pulled up outside a jeweller's shop. The driver pointed to a side door, grinning happily. I paid and over tipped him and watched him drive away before I pushed open the door and began to mount steep stairs that brought me to a landing. Facing me was an elevator. I took it to the top floor. As it came to rest, I slid my hand inside my jacket and eased the gun a little in its holster. Then I stepped across the landing to a red-painted door. I rang the bell.

There was a slight delay, then the door swung open. A Chinese girl looked inquiringly at me.

She was tall and slim and very pretty. She wore a cream silk, heavily embroidered Cheongsam and scarlet sandals. Her black hair was adorned with two lotus blossoms.

"I'm Ryan," I said. "I think you're expecting me."

She smiled, showing brilliantly white teeth.

"Yes . . . come in."

I moved into a large room full of flowers and furnished with modern light oak furniture. The big windows had a view of the sea.

"You're Mu Hai Ton?" I asked as she closed the door and walked with easy grace to an armchair.

"That is my name."

She sat down, resting her slim hands in her lap, her eyebrows slightly raised, the smile in place.

"How do I know that?"

The question seemed to amuse her. She waved a hand to the table.

"My papers are there."

I checked her identity card. She had arrived in Hong Kong five years ago. Her age was twenty-three. Her profession was that of a dancer.

I relaxed a little and sat opposite her.

"You knew Herman Jefferson?" I asked.

She nodded, continuing to smile.

"Yes, I knew him. He died two weeks ago."

"You knew his wife?"

"Yes, of course. I was a witness when they married."

"Do you know what Jefferson did for a living?"

"Perhaps now I have answered some of your questions, you will tell me who you are and why you have come here," she said, still not losing the friendly smile.

"I'm making inquiries for Jefferson's father," I told her. "He wants to know more about how his son lived out here."

She lifted her eyebrows inquiringly.

"Why?"

"I don't know. He's paying me to get the information so I'm trying to get it. I'm willing to pay you for any information you can give me."

She cocked her head on one side.

"How much will you pay?"

"It depends on how much you can tell me."

"You want to know how he made a living?" She grimaced. "He didn't make a living. He took money from Jo-An."

"Ever know a girl called Leila?"

"Yes . . . she lived with Jo-An."

"Leila told me Jefferson rented a luxury villa out at Repulse Bay."

She threw her head back and laughed. She had a nice laugh and her throat was very beautiful.

"He couldn't even afford to pay the rent at the Celestial Empire. He was no good . . . a bum."

"I heard he was tied up in the drug trade," I said casually.

That got a reaction. She stiffened and her smile went away. She stared at me, recovered herself, and shrugged.

"I know nothing about the drug trade."

"I didn't say you did. Did you ever hear he was running heroin from Canton into Hong Kong?"

"No."

"Frank Belling did it."

"I don't know anything about that." She was watching me closely now, a little frown furrowing her forehead.

"You knew Belling, didn't you?"

"I met him once . . . at the wedding."

"He was Jefferson's friend?"

"I suppose so. I don't know anything about him."

"I heard after the marriage, Jefferson left his wife and hired this villa at Repulse Bay."

She moved restlessly.

"He lived with her at the Celestial Empire until he was killed," she said. "He never had a villa at Repulse Bay."

I offered her a cigarette, but she refused. As I lit up I asked myself why I was pursuing this line of questioning. Everyone I had met and questioned had said the same thing except Leila. Why should I instinctively feel Leila was telling the truth and all the others were lying?

"Let's talk about Jo-Ann," I said. "Did you know her well?"

She nodded.

"She is one of my best friends. I am very sad she has gone to America. I hope soon to hear from her. She promised if she could arrange it for me to go there too."

I hesitated for a moment, then decided to go all the way.

"You haven't heard then?" I asked.

She looked inquiringly at me.

"Heard . . . what?"

"She's dead."

She started back as if I had slapped her face. Her eyes opened very wide and she put her hands to her breasts. I was watching her carefully. She wasn't play-acting. What I had just told her had come as a violent shock.

"Dead? How can she be dead?" she said huskily. "What happened?"

"She was murdered a few hours after arriving at Pasadena City."

Her face suddenly fell apart. There was no other description for it. Her face crumpled and she didn't look pretty any more.

"You're lying!" she said in a muffled strangled voice.

"It's a fact. The police are trying to find her killer."

She began to cry, holding her face in her hands.

"Go away," she moaned. "Please go away."

"Take it easy," I said. "I'm sorry to have given you a shock. I'm trying to find her killer myself and you could help me. Now, listen . . ."

She jumped to her feet and ran into another room, slamming the door. I stood for a moment hesitating, then I went out and closed the front door. I got in the elevator and rode down to the next floor, then getting out I waited, listening. I heard her front door open, there was a pause, then it shut. I went up the stairs silently and listened outside the red-painted door. After a few minutes I heard the tinkle of the telephone bell. I heard her talking softly and rapidly, but too softly to hear what she was saying. When she hung up, I went down the stairs to the elevator and took it to the ground floor. I walked out onto the crowded bustling street. Across the way was an arcade of shops. I entered and stood looking at various complicated cameras offered at give-away prices, my eyes from time to time looking at the door to the apartments opposite I could see reflected in the mirror in the showcase. I was acting on a hunch, but after ten minutes of waiting, I began to wonder if the hunch was going to pay off. Then just as I was about to give up, I saw her come out into the street. If I hadn't been watching carefully I wouldn't have recognised her. She was now wearing the drab black costume of the working peasant: the short coat and the baggy trousers. She looked to right and left and then walked quickly away towards the waterfront. I went after her. She was easy enough to follow. She reached a taxi rank, spoke to the driver, then got in. The taxi edged its way into the traffic.

I was lucky. The driver of the second taxi in the rank could understand a little English. I told him to follow the taxi ahead and showed him a twenty-dollar bill. He grinned cheerfully, nodded and as soon as I was in his cab, he went after the taxi which was now fifty yards ahead.

Mu Hai Ton got out at the Star Ferry station. I gave her a head start, then paid off my driver and went after her. She went third-class and I went first. The ferry-boat took us to the Kowloon City pier which is close to the Kai Tak airport.

From the ferry station she took a rickshaw. I decided it would be safer and easier to follow her on foot, but I had misjudged the speed a rickshaw boy can travel and I nearly lost her. By running hard, stared at by the Chinese who must have thought I was crazy, I just managed to hang on to the rickshaw, but only just.

She left the rickshaw in a narrow street, swarming with vendors, rickshaws and coolies trotting along with their heavy burdens and I watched her enter an alley that I knew led into the old walled City of Kowloon.

This part of Hong Kong was in actual fact Red Chinese territory. At one time the British authorities had no right to enter it, and it had become a sanctuary for criminals and drug addicts. But now, conditions having become so bad, the police made a regular patrol, and there had been no protest from the Red Chinese Government. But it wasn't a place where any European would want to go.

I went after her. In the narrow crowded alleys with their stinking open drains, there was no hope of quick concealment. If she had looked back she would have seen me, but she didn't. I kept twenty yards behind her, jostling the filthy-looking Chinese who stared at me with drug bemused eyes, moving away from me as if I were something untouchable.

We walked some distance through a maze of horrible alleys, then she paused at a door, pushed it open and went into a house. I waited a moment, aware I was being watched by a number of Chinese who either squatted or leaned against the wall of the alley, their faces the colour of mushroom fungus, the pupils of their eyes like pinpoints. I didn't believe they even saw me, but their fixed stare gave me the creeps.

I pushed open the door. Facing me was a steep, narrow flight of uncarpeted stairs. I moved in and closed the door. I listened. Somewhere above I could hear a woman's voice. I eased my gun in its holster, then went silently up the stairs to a landing. Facing me was a door. To my right was another door.

I paused, listening. I heard a man say, "Listen, you yellow bitch . . . if you're lying to me, I'll kill you!" The accent was American: the tone vicious.

"That's what he said!" Mu Hai Ton's voice was shrill. "He said she was murdered a few hours after she had arrived in Pasadena City!"

A gentle voice said behind me, "Don't move, Mr. Ryan. Just keep your hands still if you please."

A familiar voice with a heavy Chinese accent that I couldn't place.

I remained still because in spite of the polite tone, the threat was there.

"Please open the door and go in. I have a gun in my hand."

I took a step forward, turned the door handle and gave the door a little push. It swung wide open.

It was a bare room. The floor was uncarpeted. There was a broad wooden bench that served as a bed with a wooden headrest to serve as a pillow. On an upturned packing case stood a metal kettle burned black, a small teapot and some small dirty tea bowls. Hanging on a hook on the wall was a filthy hand towel and below it was a basin and a large water jug.

The two figures squatting on the floor turned to stare at me. One of them was Mu Hai Ton. The other was a narrow-shouldered, lean-faced man, wearing a dirty black Chinese costume and a baggy black cap pulled down over his face.

For a brief moment I took him for Chinese, but a closer look told me he was European.

Mu Hai Ton gave a startled scream. The man swung his arm and the back of his hand caught her across the mouth, knocking her sprawling at my feet.

"You stupid bitch!" the man snarled, getting to his feet. "You led him right here! Get out!"

"Go on in, please," the voice said behind me and I received a gentle prod in the back.

The girl scrambled to her feet, sobbing. She darted around me and I heard her clattering down the stairs.

I moved into the room. The man was staring at me, a vicious, cold gleam in his eyes.

I took a chance and glanced over my shoulder. Wong Hop Ho, the English-speaking guide, smiled apologetically at me. In his right hand he held a .45 Colt centred on my spine. He closed the door and set his back against it.

I examined the man before me. He looked half-starved and ill. He was unshaven and dirty and I could smell him.

"See if he has a gun," the man said.

Wong pressed his gun into my spine. With his left hand he patted me over, found my gun and removed it. He then stood away.

I decided this man in front of me could be no one else but Frank Belling. If he wasn't then nothing else made sense.

"Are you Belling?" I said. "I've been looking for you."

"Okay, so you've found me," the man said. "It's going to do you damn little good."

I looked at Wong who continued to smile apologetically at me.

"I certainly fell for you," I said ruefully. "You were waiting at the airport to pick me up. That was careless of me. Who tipped you off I was coming?"

Wong giggled.

"We hear these things," he said. "You shouldn't have been so curious, Mr. Ryan. You certainly shouldn't have come here."

"Well, I'm here," I said. "I can't help it if I'm curious . . . it's my business to be curious."

"What do you want?" Belling demanded.

"I'm trying to find out why Jo-An Jefferson was murdered. The idea was I should start from here and work back."

His eyes glittered wolfishly in his thin pale face.

"Is that straight . . . she's dead?"

"Yes . . . she's dead."

He took off his baggy cap and threw it aside. His sand-coloured hair needed cutting. He ran filthy fingers through his hair and his mouth tightened into a thin line.

"What happened to her?" he said. "Come on . . . give me the facts."

I told him about the mysterious telephone caller, John Hardwick, how I had been fooled into leaving my office, how I had found her dead on my return. I told him old man Jefferson had hired me to find her killer.

"He said his son would have wanted to find the man who killed her. He felt it was the least he could do to do what his son would have done."

Belling said: "What are the police doing? Can't they find him?"

99

"They're getting nowhere. I'm getting nowhere either. That's why I was looking for you."

"Why the hell do you imagine I could help you?" he demanded, glaring at me. Sweat was running down his thin, white face. He looked frightened and vicious.

"You could tell me something about Jefferson," I said. "Was he hooked up in this drug organisation you belong to?"

"I don't know a thing about Jefferson! You keep out of this! Now get out! Jefferson is dead. Let him stay dead. Go on, get out!"

I should have been more alert, but I wasn't and I suffered for it. I saw Belling look past me at Wong. I spun around. Wong stabbed me in the belly with his gun barrel. As I jerked forward in agony, he slammed the gun butt down on top of my head.

3

I heard myself saying silently, "Frank Belling is English, isn't he?" and a voice that sounded like the voice of Chief Inspector MacCarthy replied, "That's right . . . he's English."

And yet the thin, dirty specimen who said he was Frank Belling had spoken with a strong American accent. Was it possible an Englishman could have picked up such an accent? I didn't think so.

A sudden stab of pain in my head concluded these thoughts and I heard myself groan.

"All right . . . all right," I said aloud. "You're not hurt all that bad. You've just had a bang on the head. You have to expect that in your business. You're lucky to be alive."

I opened my eyes. I could see nothing. It was as dark as a tunnel, but the familiar smell told me I was still in the room where Wong had coshed me. I sat up slowly, wincing at more stabbing pains and I gently felt the bump on my head. I sat there for some minutes, then I made the effort and got to my feet. The door would be behind me and to the left. I groped my way to it, found the door handle and opened the door. A feeble light burning on the landing made me blink. I stood in the doorway listening, but heard only the gentle murmur of many voices in the alley below. I looked at my strap watch. The time was five minutes past midnight. I had been unconscious for about half an hour . . . quite long enough for Belling and Wong to have got well away.

My one thought now was to get out of this evil-smelling hole.

As I started towards the stairs, I heard someone coming up. I slid my hand inside my coat. The gun holster was there still strapped to my side, but it was empty.

The beam of a powerful flashlight hit me in the face.

"What do you think you're doing here?" a familiar Scottish voice demanded.

"Slumming," I said and relaxed. "What are you?"

Sergeant Hamish, followed by a uniformed Chinese police officer, came on up the stairs.

"You were spotted coming in here," he said. "I thought I'd better see what you were up to."

"You're a little late. I've been holding a one-sided conversation with your pal Frank Belling."

"You were?" He gaped at me. "Where is he?"

"He's skipped." I fingered the lump on the back of my head. "A Chinese pal of his boffed me before we had time to exchange confidences."

He moved the beam of his flashlight so he could see the back of my head, then he whistled.

"Well, you asked for it, coming here. This is the toughest spot in Hong Kong."

"Would you take that goddam light out of my eyes? My head hurts," I growled at him.

He moved past me into the room and swung the light around. Then he came out.

"The Chief Inspector will want to talk to you. Let's go."

"He'll want to talk to a Chinese girl named Mu Hai Ton too," I said and gave him the girl's address. "You'd better get after her. She's likely to have skipped."

"What's she got to do with this?"

"She led me to Belling. Hurry it up, friend. You could miss her."

He said something in Cantonese to the policeman with him who clattered off down the stairs.

"You come on," he said to me and we followed the policeman into the dark, evil-smelling alley.

Half an hour later I was back on the island and sitting in Chief Inspector MacCarthy's office. They had got him out of bed by radio-telephone and he looked none too pleased. We had cups of strong tea in front of us. My head was still aching but the tea helped.

Sergeant Hamish leaned against the wall, chewing a tooth-pick, his cop eyes blankly staring at me. MacCarthy sucked at his empty pipe while he listened to my story.

I didn't tell him about the Silver Mine Bay outing. I felt if I had told him he might have turned hostile. I told him how I had wanted to talk to Mu Hai Ton, how I had found her through the Madame at the Wanchai bar and how I had seen her surprise and distress when I had told her Jo-An was dead.

"I had an idea she might want to pass on the news," I said, "so I waited across the road and followed her into the walled city."

I told them how Wong had suddenly appeared, what Belling had said and how Wong had coshed me.

After a long pause, MacCarthy said, "Well, you asked for it. You should have come to me."

I let that one go.

He sat for some moments thinking over what I had told him, then before he could say what was on his mind, the telephone bell rang. He scooped up the receiver, listened, then said, "Well, keep after her, I want her," and hung up.

"She didn't return to her apartment," he said to me. "I have a man watching the place and we're looking for her."

I hadn't expected she would have been there waiting for them to pick her up. I wondered if they would eventually find her in the harbour the way they had found Leila.

"Have you a photograph of Frank Belling?" I asked. "I have an idea this guy wasn't Belling. He was an American."

MacCarthy opened a desk drawer and took out a fat file which showed he was taking more interest in Belling than he had led me to believe. He opened the file and took out a half-plate glossy print which he flicked across the desk so it fell right side up in front of me.

I looked at the photograph and felt a queer creepy sensation crawl up my spine. It was the same photograph that Janet West had given me: the hard gangster face Janet West had said belonged to Herman Jefferson.

"You sure this is Belling?" I said.

MacCarthy stared blankly at me.

"That's a police photograph. We distributed a number of them to the newspaper agencies and to the newspapers when we were trying to pick him up. Yes . . . that's Frank Belling."

"That's not the man I talked to . . . the man who said he was Frank Belling."

MacCarthy drank some of his tea and then began to fill his pipe. I could see by the expression in his eyes he was beginning to dislike me.

"Then who was the man you talked to?"

"Did you ever meet Herman Jefferson?"

"Yes . . . why?"

"Got a photograph of him?"

"No . . . he was an American citizen. Why should I have a photograph of him?"

"Can you describe him?"

"Thin, sharp-featured with thinning sand-coloured hair," MacCarthy said promptly.

"Sound like the man I talked to . . . the man who said he was Frank Belling."

There was a long pause, then MacCarthy said heavily, "Jefferson is dead. He was killed in a road accident and his body was shipped to America."

"Jefferson is alive . . . anyway, he was alive two hours ago," I said. "That description of yours fits him."

"The body in the car matched Jefferson's size," MacCarthy said as if trying to convince himself. "The body was so badly burned identification wasn't possible but his wife identified him by the ring on his finger and the cigarette case he was carrying. We had and still have no reason to think he was anyone else but Jefferson."

"If it wasn't Jefferson and I'm damn sure it wasn't, who was it?" I said.

"Why ask me?" MacCarthy said. "I've still no reason to think Jefferson is alive."

"A tall thin man with pale green eyes, thin sandy hair and thin lips," I said. I thought for a moment, then went on, "He had a crooked little finger on his right hand, come to think of it, as if it had been broken at one time and had been badly set."

"That's Jefferson," Hamish said. It was the first time he had said anything since I had come into the office. "I remember the crooked finger. That's Jefferson all right."

MacCarthy puffed at his pipe.

"Then who was buried?" he asked uneasily. "Whose body was sent back to America?"

"My guess is that it was Frank Belling's body," I said. "For some reason Jefferson tried to kid me he was Belling."

"Why should he do that?"

"I don't know." I touched the bump on my head and grimaced. "If it's all the same to you, Chief Inspector, I'll go to bed. I'm feeling like something the cat has dragged in."

"You look like it," he said. "Let's have a description of Wong."

"He looks like any other Chinese to me. Squat, fat with gold teeth."

"That's right," MacCarthy said and stifled a yawn. "They all look alike to us just as we all look alike to them." He turned to Hamish. "Take as many men as you want and go through the walled city. See if you can find Jefferson. You won't, but we've got to try." To me, he said, "Okay, Ryan, you go to bed. You can leave this to us."

I said I would be glad to and went out of the office with Hamish.

"Looking for Jefferson in the walled city is like looking for the invisible man," Hamish said bitterly. "No one knows anything. Everyone covers up for everyone. I might have Jefferson right next to me and I wouldn't know it."

"Cheer up," I said unfeelingly. "It'll give you something to do."

Leaving him swearing, I picked up the Packard and drove back to the Repulse Bay Hotel. I felt old, tired and worn out.

I left the elevator on the fourth floor where my room was. The night boy, a grinning, bowing Chinese, wearing a white drill jacket and black trousers, bowed to me as he handed me my key. I thanked him and walked to my room. I unlocked the door and entered the sitting-room. Most of the rooms in the hotel had sitting-rooms. The bedroom was beyond drawn curtains that divided the two rooms. I turned on the light and pulled off my jacket. The air-conditioner made the room pleasantly cool.

My one thought was to take a cold shower and then go to bed, but it wasn't to be. As I parted the curtains and moved into the bedroom, I saw the bedside lamp was on.

I saw a woman lying on the bed. It was Stella Enright. She had on a gold and black cocktail dress. She had kicked off her shoes that were lying by the bed.

The sight of her gave me a shock. For a moment I thought she was dead, then I saw she was breathing by the rise and fall of her breasts. I stood there, staring at her, aware of the pain in my head and wondering what the hell she was doing here and how she got in. Then I remembered the grinning night boy and guessed she had bribed her way in.

As I watched her, she slowly opened her eyes and looked at me, then she lifted her head. Sitting up, she swung her long legs off the bed.

"I'm sorry," she said and smiled. "I didn't mean to fall asleep. I just got bored waiting for you."

"Have you been waiting long?" I asked, more for something to say. I sat down in an armchair, watching her as she slipped into her shoes. She patted her hair and then stood up and came into the sitting-room.

"I've been here since ten o'clock," she said. "I was worrying about you. I hope you don't mind me coming here." She hurried on before I could say anything. "What happened to you? I nearly missed the ferry. Why weren't you waiting for me?"

"I was delayed," I said, thinking of the thin Chinese with his knife and the squat Chinese with his rifle. "Now I'll ask you something. Was it your idea that you and I should go to Silver Mine Bay?"

She sat on the arm of the armchair facing me.

"My idea? What do you mean?"

"It's not so hard, surely? When you suggested I should see the waterfall . . . was it your idea or did someone else suggest it to you?"

She frowned, staring at me for a moment, then she said, "I don't know why you ask, but my brother told me to invite you. He said you were lonely and would be glad of company."

"Is he your brother?" I asked.

She stiffened, stared at me and then quickly looked away.

As she said nothing, I repeated the question.

"You're asking the most extraordinary questions," she said, still looking away from me. "What makes you ask that?"

"There's no likeness between you," I said, "and it seems odd to me that a girl like you should want to live with her brother."

I watched her hesitate, then she shrugged.

"No, he isn't my brother. I've only known him a couple of months. Now, I'm sorry I ever met him."

I gave up the thought of going to bed. I took out my pack of cigarettes and we both lit up. She slid off the arm of the chair into the chair itself and leaning back, she closed her eyes, inhaling deeply.

"Where did you meet him?" I asked.

"In Singapore. I was doing a strip act at a night club there," she told me. "I'd come all the way from New York . . . like the dope I am. The night club was raided and I never got my money and I was strapped. Harry turned up. He had seen my act several times and he propositioned me. He had plenty of money, certain charm and . . . well, I went to live with him in a bungalow near the MacRitchie reservoir. It was nice out there. I had a good time with him until people began to talk, then it wasn't so good." She opened her eyes to stare at the burning tip of her cigarette. "I decided to go home, but Harry wouldn't give me the fare. Then suddenly he had to come here. He got me a false passport. We came here as brother and sister." She looked at me. "I still want to go home. Could you lend me the money? I'll pay you back in a couple of months."

"How did he get you a false passport?"

She shook her head.

"I don't know . . I didn't ask. Will you lend me the money?"

"I never lend that kind of money."

"If it would make any difference, we could travel together." She smiled stiffly at me. I had a sudden idea she was frightened. There was a bleak, scared expression in her eyes. "You know what I mean . . . value for money."

"I want a drink," I said. "Will you have one?"

She sat bolt upright, her eyes widening.

"Don't let anyone in here," she said, her voice going shrill. "I don't want anyone to know I'm here."

"The boy knows. He let you in, didn't he?"

"No. I got the number of your room and took the key off the board. There were two keys. He doesn't know I'm here."

I wished my head would stop aching.

"What are you scared about?"

She relaxed back in the chair, looking away from me.

"I'm not scared. I just want to get away from here. I want to go home."

"Why the sudden urgency?"

"Must you ask so many questions? Will you lend me the money? I'll sleep with you now it you'll promise to give me the money."

"I'll give you the money if you'll tell me all you know about Harry Enright."

I saw her hesitate, then she said, "I know very little about him really. He's just a playboy having himself a good time."

I was too tired to be patient.

"Well, if that's all you know I'll keep my money," I said and getting to my feet I crossed to the telephone. "I'm going to order a drink and then I'm going to bed . . . alone. You'd better get out before the waiter comes."

"No . . . wait."

I called room service and asked for a bottle of Scotch and ice. As I replaced the receiver, she got to her feet.

"Will you really give me the money if I tell you what I know about him?"

"That's what I said."

"I think he is a drug smuggler," she said, clenching and unclenching her hands.

"Why do you think that?"

"People come to see him at night. When we were in Singapore he used to go down to the docks and meet sailors. The police once raided our bungalow in Singapore and they searched the place, but they didn't find anything. Here, we get night visitors. They are always Chinese. He goes out in the early hours in his boat."

"Jefferson did live in your villa before you came?"

"Yes. Harry told me not to tell you. When Jefferson was killed, Harry was sent from Singapore to replace him. The villa is conveniently situated for receiving drugs."

There came a gentle tap on the door.

"That's the waiter," I said. "Get into the bathroom and stay quiet."

As soon as she was in the bathroom and had shut the door, I went across the room to let the waiter in.

Just outside the door, smiling, was Harry Enright. He had a .38 automatic in his hand which he pointed at me.

"Don't start anything smart, pal," he said. "Just back in and keep your hands still."

I backed in, keeping my hands still.

"Don't look so hopeful," Enright said, closing the door and leaning against it. "I told the waiter you had changed your mind . . . he's gone away."

"Okay for me to sit down?" I said. "The excitement is getting too much for me."

I sat down, keeping my hands on my knees and I studied him. The smile was fixed. There was a cold, vicious expression in his eyes that warned me to be careful. The gun was steady in his hand and the sight was centred on a spot just between my eyes.

"You're smart," Enright said. "You don't know how goddam smart you are. You did something I haven't been able to do for the past three weeks."

"What would that be?" I asked.

"You found Jefferson. I've been hunting for that son-of-a-bitch until I thought I'd go crazy. To think I nearly had you killed! Then you go out and find him . . . just like that."

"I'm not following you," I said. "Do you have to point that gun at me? I've had a heavy day and that gun looks lethal."

Still keeping me covered, he moved farther into the room. He sat on the same chair arm on which Stella had sat not ten minutes ago.

"Don't worry about the gun," he said. "Just so long as you don't start anything smart, you won't get a bullet in your head. What did you tell the cops?"

"What makes you imagine I told the cops anything?"

"I've had a man on your tail from the moment you started showing interest in the villa. I spotted you in the pedallo. From that moment we haven't taken our eyes off you."

"We? You mean this drug traffic organisation?"

"That's it, pal. It's a big thing . . . too big for you. It makes me sweat to think those two might have killed you. That was my mistake. I should have left you alone. I had no idea you were after Jefferson."

"I wasn't . . . I thought he was dead."

"We thought he was too. He nearly had us fooled. We were hunting for Belling. Then you come along and you led us right to Jefferson."

"So you found him," I said, wondering what Stella was doing, shut in the bathroom.

"Yes, we found him." His smile was vicious. "We found Wong too."

"Who is Wong?"

"He was one of our group, but he made the mistake of throwing in with Jefferson. Right at this moment they are getting the treatment, then what's left of them will be dumped in the sea."

"What did they do to you then?"

"That's the way we treat hijackers," Enright said. "It's the only way. What did you tell the cops?"

"Nothing they didn't know already," I said mildly.

He stared at me for a long moment, then he stood up.

"You and me are going for a little walk and then a little drive. There are four of my men outside. You make one move out of turn and it'll be your last move. My boys carry knives. They can kill a guy from forty feet. By the time anyone knows you're dead, they'll be miles away: so watch it. Come on, let's go."

"What happens after the walk and the drive?" I asked.

He grinned at me.

"You'll find out. Up on your feet, pal, and watch it."

I stood up as he backed to the door. He opened it and stood aside.

"The night boy won't help you. He works for me, so don't act foolish," Enright said. "We'll walk down the stairs. There's another of my boys in the lobby. Just keep moving if you want to keep alive."

We went out into the passage. Enright had put the gun in his pocket, his hand gripping the gun. The night boy grinned at me as we walked to the head of the stairs.

"Go on down," Enright said. "I'm right behind you."

I plodded down four flights of stairs and into the big lobby.

It was strangely deserted. Only two men sat in lounging chairs. One of them was Sergeant Hamish. The other had cop written all over him. I hadn't seen him before. I took one look at them and then flung myself face down on the plush carpet a split second before a gun roared behind me. I lay there, my heart hammering as more gunfire crashed above me.

After a while, a shoe prodded me.

"You can get up," Hamish said.

I rolled over and looked up at him, then I got slowly to my feet. Enright was lying on his back, blood running from a wound in his face. His jacket was smoking. A second look at him told me he was dead.

"Did you have to kill him?" I asked.

"If I hadn't he would have killed you," Hamish said indifferently. "Maybe he would even have killed me."

"There are others and the night boy on the fourth floor is one of them."

The other cop started for the elevator as Hamish said, "We've bagged the others. Who was the woman who telephoned us?"

I looked blankly at him.

"Was there a woman?"

"How the hell should we be here if she hadn't told us what was going on?" Hamish said irritably. "A woman telephoned. Who was she?"

"I wouldn't know," I said. "Maybe one of my fans."

Half a dozen Chinese policemen came into the lobby. Hamish spoke to them, then jerked his head at me.

"Come on," he said. "You'll have to talk to the Chief Inspector."

As the Chinese policemen were gathering up what was left of Enright, Hamish and I went out to the waiting jeep.

I remained in a room at police headquarters for more than three hours. It had a couch in it and I slept. Around four o'clock in the morning, Hamish, looking bleak and tired, shook me awake.

"Come on," he said.

I groaned, aware my head was still aching, and sat up.

"What's cooking now?" I asked.

"The Chief Inspector is ready to talk to you. Why should you be the only one to sleep?"

MacCarthy was puffing away at his pipe, a cup of tea within reach. A police officer put a cup of tea by me as I eased myself stiffly onto the upright chair. Hamish, struggling with a yawn, lolled against the wall.

"The marine police picked up a man trying to get away in Enright's speedboat," MacCarthy said. "We had some trouble with him, but he's finally let the cat out of the bag."

"An American?"

"Chinese . . . he comes from Canton. As you're working on the Jefferson case I thought I'd fill you in."

"Thanks. Has Jefferson been found yet?"

"He was fished out of the bay about half an hour ago," Mac-Carthy said and grimaced. "I bet he wished he had died the first time. They certainly roughed him up before they killed him. We now have the facts of the case clear. The way I see it is this: ever since Jefferson arrived here he has been living on the immoral earnings of this girl, Jo-An. I don't know why he eventually married her unless it was to stop her mouth, but anyway, he married her a few weeks after he first met Frank Belling who, as I told you, was one of the chief operators in this drug smuggling racket. Belling had this villa at Repulse Bay, rented from Lin Fan. Whether Lin Fan had any idea how the villa was being used is something I don't know, but I intend to find out if I can. The villa was convenient for landing consignments of drugs. There was a harbour, a speedboat, and it was isolated. But things began to get too hot for Belling. We were getting a warrant for his arrest. He was tipped off that we were closing in on him and he decided to skip to Canton until things cooled off. But someone had to be at the villa to take care of the delivery of drugs. He persuaded Jefferson to go there. Not that Jefferson would have needed much persuasion. By going there, he would be living in luxury. He walked out on Jo-An and moved into the villa. Belling went to Canton. An arrangement was made to bring in over two thousand ounces of heroin. Belling came to the villa by night to explain to Jefferson how the delivery was to be made. That amout of heroin is worth a fortune in the right hands. Jefferson began to wonder if he could steal it, but he didn't know how to get rid of it once he had it, and he was also scared the organisation would catch him. However fate, if you like to call it that, played into his hands. The heroin arrived and was stored in the villa. Belling and Jefferson drove out to Lecky Pass which is a jumping-off place into Canton. On the way, there was an accident and Belling was killed. Jefferson saw his chance. He put his ring on Belling's finger, planted his cigarette case in Belling's pocket and then set fire to the car. The scene of the accident was a lonely spot and the time was four o'clock in the morning, so no one disturbed Jefferson. He got back to the villa by stealing a bicycle and he removed the heroin which he took possibly to the Celestial Empire Hotel. I'm talking more or less off the cuff now, but I am sure he persuaded his wife to identify Belling's body as his. Then he went into hiding in the walled City of Kowloon."

"Why did he do that?" I asked.

"This was a rushed job. The opportunity presented itself and he grabbed at it, but he found he was stuck with it. The organisation was quick off the mark. As soon as the accident was reported they sent one of their men to the villa to find the heroin had vanished. Naturally, they thought Belling had hijacked the consignment and they began searching for him. This was a piece of luck for Jefferson. So long as the organisation thought Belling was their man, Jefferson was in the clear. But he had to get out of Hong Kong. This found impossible. He was supposed to be dead and he hadn't the means of laying his hands on a false passport. So he was stuck."

"And the heroin?" I asked.

MacCarthy frowned.

"I have an idea we'll never find it. It's my bet from the state of Jefferson's body when we found him, they had persuaded him to tell them where he had hidden it."

"What puzzles me is why Jo-An took the trouble to take Belling's body back to Jefferson's father," I said.

"She had to get out of Hong Kong. She had no money. By bringing the body back, she got the fare from old man Jefferson," MacCarthy said.

"Yeah . . . I guess that's right. How about Wong?"

"He was one of them of course and he made the mistake of throwing in with Jefferson."

"He was there to meet me at the airport. How did he know I was coming? He must have been tipped off by someone—but who? When I used him as an interpreter, he led me right up the garden path. His job was obviously to keep me away from Jefferson and he nearly succeeded. If it hadn't been for Leila we would never have got onto Enright."

"Will Jefferson want the body sent back?"

"I guess so. I'll see Wilcox at the American Consulate and fix up the necessary papers. Has Wong's body been found?"

"We're still fishing for him. This Chinese we caught said both bodies were jumped in the same place."

I looked admiringly at him.

"You must have been very persuasive. This guy seems to have sung like a skylark."

MacCarthy rubbed the side of his nose with the bowl of his pipe.

"The Chinese aren't kind to each other," he said. "The marine police had him for half an hour before they turned him over to me. He tried to stick one of them with a knife. They got a little rough with him."

"That's pretty fast work to have softened him to that extent."

"Yes, they work fast." He seemed bored with this topic. Casually, he asked, "By the way, you wouldn't know about a Chinese found shot out at Silver Mine Bay, would you? He was shot through the head with a Lee-Enfield rifle."

"He was? I haven't handled a Lee-Enfield since I left the infantry."

"I wasn't suggesting you shot him. You were out there this afternoon?"

"Come to think of it, I was. I had a look at the waterfall."

"That's where the body was found."

"Isn't that extraordinary?"

"You heard no shooting?"

"Not a thing."

MacCarthy stared at me, then shrugged his shoulders.

"I was pretty sure you would have reported a shooting if you had known about it."

"You're absolutely right."

There was a long pause while Hamish took out his pipe and began to fill it.

"Enright had a sister," MacCarthy said. "Rather a glamorous piece. Would you know where she is?"

"At the villa I suppose, in bed where I'd like to be."

"She's not there . . . we've looked. When did you last see her?"

"On the ferry-boat going to Silver Mine Bay. She was taking groceries to an old ex-servant. We travelled together."

"You haven't seen her since?"

"Can't say I have."

"I had the idea she was the woman who tipped us that Enright was in your room."

"She could have done. She has a nice nature."

MacCarthy suddenly smiled.

"Come off it, Ryan. We've checked on her. Her name is Stella May Tyson. She is a stripper who worked at a night club in

111

Singapore. She and Enright joined up. She came here with a forged passport."

"And so?" I asked, looking steadily at him.

"When she telephoned we traced the call to the hotel. They told us she called from the bathroom in your suite. She was seen going up the stairs towards your suite at ten o'clock. I think she's still in your suite."

"She probably is . . . I hope so," I said. "She saved my life. What do you expect me to do . . . hand her over to you?"

"It's not a wise thing to tell lies to police officers," MacCarthy said as he began to clean his pipe with a gull's feather, "but as she saved your life and as she has given us the opportunity of breaking up this drug organisation, I think we can forget about her. Tell her if she gets out by tomorrow night and stays out, we won't make trouble for her. She has twenty-four hours to get out. If she is still here after that time, then we'll have to do something about her."

"Thanks," I said. "I'll tell her. I'm getting out myself. There's nothing more here I can do. I've still to find out who murdered Jefferson's wife. Whoever did it is in Pasadena City. With what I have found out here, I should be able to find the killer. Okay for me to leave now?"

"It's all right with me," MacCarthy said.

"I guess I'll go back to the hotel now and get me some sleep!"

"If that girl is still in your room, I don't imagine you'll get much sleep," MacCarthy said with a sly grin.

"What a mind you've got," I said, getting to my feet. "How about sending me back by car?"

MacCarthy turned to Hamish.

"Send him back by car. He's in a hurry," he said, and pulling a file towards him, he settled down to work.

I got back to the Repulse Bay Hotel as the sun was beginning to creep up behind the mountains. I went up to my room, took the key from a grinning Chinese I hadn't seen before and unlocked my door.

The light was on. Stella was dozing in an armchair. She started up as I came in, her eyes scared.

"Relax," I said, shutting and locking the door. "There's nothing now for you to be scared about."

"What happened? I heard shooting. I thought they had killed you."

I flopped into an armchair.

"You did me a good turn . . . thanks."

"I had to do something. I was terrified he would hear me telephoning."

"Well, you've got your wish . . . you can leave for home within the next twenty-four hours. I'll pay the fare. The police won'

112

worry you. You'd better use your own passport. Have you still got it?"

She drew in a long deep breath.

"Yes, I've got it. And Harry?"

"He was unlucky. The police were better shots. It's the best way out for him. He wouldn't have taken to jail life."

She shuddered.

"He's dead?"

"Yes, he's dead. I want some sleep. I'm going to take a shower and then I'm going to sleep. You have the bed. I'll take the settee."

I shut myself in the bathroom and took a shower. I was feeling pretty old and pretty worn out. I put on my pyjamas and came out of the bathroom.

She was waiting for me. She had stripped off her clothes and was lying on the bed. We looked at each other, then she held out her arms. She was still holding me in her arms, sometime later, when I fell asleep.

CHAPTER FOUR

1

IT all seemed very familiar . . . the smell of sweat, disinfectant and fear; the green painted corridor, the tramp of heavy feet, the stony-faced cops who shoved past me as if I didn't exist.

I paused outside Detective Lieutenant Retnick's door and knocked.

A voice bawled something. I turned the handle and went in.

Retnick was sitting at his desk. Detective Sergeant Pulski leaned against the wall, chewing a matchstick.

They both stared at me, then Retnick pushed his hat to the back of his head and slapped his blotter with a well-manicured hand.

"Look who's here," he said to no one in particular. "Well, what a surprise! If I'd known you were coming, I'd have turned out the town band. Sit down. What were the Chinese tarts like?"

"I wouldn't know," I said, sitting down. "I've been too busy to find out. Got the murder case solved yet?"

Retnick pulled out his cigar case, selected a cigar, bit off the end and stuck the cigar into his face. He didn't offer me one.

"Not yet . . . have you got anything?"

"Could have. You haven't got one single thing?"

He lit the cigar, frowning.

"We're still trying to find Hardwick. What have you got?"

"The body that Jo-An Jefferson brought back here wasn't Herman Jefferson's."

That shook him. He choked on smoke, cursed, put down his cigar and blew his nose on a soiled handkerchief. He put the handkerchief away, then tilted back his chair and squinted at me with watering eyes.

"Look, shamus, if this isn't the McCoy, you're going to have a rought time. I mean just that."

"Herman Jefferson was murdered two days ago," I said. "He was dropped into the sea a few miles outside Hong Kong. The British police fished him out. The body is coming back by plane at the end of this week."

"For sweet Pete's sake! Who was in the coffin then?"

"No one you'd know . . . a guy named Frank Belling, a British subject, connected with heroin smuggling."

"Have you talked to old man Jefferson yet?"

"Not yet . . . you're my first port of call. He's my second."

Retnick stared at Pulski who stared blankly back at him, then Retnick shifted his gaze and stared at me.

"Give with the mouth," he said. "All of it. Hey! Wait a minute. I'll have it on paper." He picked up the telephone receiver and bawled for a stenographer. While we waited, he chewed on his cigar, scowling and worried.

A young cop came in and sat down away from us. He opened a notebook and looked expectantly at Retnick and then at me.

"Shoot," Retnick said to me. "Give me one of your classical statements, shamus. Don't leave anything out. I'm going to check every word you utter and if I find out you're lying, you'll be sorry your father had a sex life."

"I don't have to take that talk from you, Retnick," I said, suddenly angry. "Jefferson is waiting to fix you and a word from me could fix you good."

Pulski pushed himself off the wall he was holding up. The young cop looked horrified. Before Pulski could take a swing at me, Retnick was on his feet, shoving Pulski back.

"Shut up!" he snarled at Pulski. To me, he said, "Relax, shamus. Okay, so I take it back. You don't have to be so goddam sensitive. Come on, for Judas' sake, let's have the statement."

I eyed him for a long moment, but he wouldn't meet my stare, then I calmed down. I lit a cigarette and gave him the statement. I covered everything that had happened to me since I had arrived in Hong Kong. The only fact I kept quiet about was that Stella and I had returned to New York together. There we had parted. I was sorry to part with her, and she seemed sorry to part with me, but once back in her own environment there seemed no point in us continuing. She had done me a good turn and I had done her one. I had given her two hundred dollars with which to make a new start. It had been my money and not Jefferson's. She had thanked me with a rueful smile and had said goodbye. That was the last I ever saw of her.

Retnick smoked two cigars while I was talking. When I had finished, he told the young cop to get the statement typed and when he had gone, he told Pulski to take a walk.

When we were alone, Retnick said, "Still doesn't explain why the yellow skin got shot, does it?"

"It doesn't."

"I wouldn't be in your shoes having to tell that son-of-a-bitch Jefferson his son was a drug pedlar."

"Then you don't wear my shoes," I said.

"We'll have to open the coffin." Retnick lit his third cigar. "Don't suppose the old man will like that too much."

"Why shouldn't he? The coffin doesn't contain his son."

"That's right," Retnick brooded. "Better get it done fast and quietly. It'd help if you got the old man's say-so. We'll have to open the family vault."

"I'll get it."

"The newspapers will love this," Retnick said, his face gloomy. "Could be they'll stir up trouble."

"Yeah."

He brooded for some moments, then took out his cigar case and offered it to me.

"Not for me," I said. "I'm a lung cancer addict."

"Yeah . . . I was forgetting." Retnick polished the cigar case on his sleeve. "I don't want trouble, Ryan. I'm relying on you. Maybe I should have looked in the coffin before I released it."

"Someone smart is bound to bring that point up."

"Yeah . . ."

There was a long pause, then I got to my feet.

"I'll talk to Mr. Jefferson."

"I'll be waiting for you to call me. As soon as you get his okay, I'll open the coffin."

"I'll get it."

"Remember, Ryan, you can always do with a good friend at police headquarters . . . just remember that."

"Just so long as you remember me, I'll remember you. We could make a song out of that, couldn't we?"

I left him, staring uneasily into space and went down to where I had parked my car. I got under the wheel, lit a cigarette and brooded for several minutes. I decided first to go to my office just to see if it was still there. From my office I could telephone Janet West and see if the old man would be ready to talk to me this afternoon.

I drove to my office, parked and rode up in the elevator. As I unlocked my office door, I heard Jay Wayde's deep voice dictating. There was a heap of mail lying on the floor. I picked it up and dumped it on my dust-covered desk. Then, as I found the room stuffy, I crossed to the window and opened it wide. Jay Wayde's baritone voice came clearly to me. He was dictating a letter about a consignment of adhesive plaster. I listened for a brief moment before moving back to my desk. I flicked through my mail which seemed depressingly non-productive. Only three letters looked like business: the rest were circulars which I dumped into the trash-basket.

I reached for the telephone and called J. Wilbur Jefferson's residence. The voice of the gloomy butler asked who was calling. I told him. There was a delay, then Janet West came on the line.

"This is Mr. Jefferson's secretary. Is that Mr. Ryan?"

I said it was, then, "Can I see Mr. Jefferson?"

"Yes, of course. Will you come at three o'clock this afternoon?"

"I'll be there."

"Have you found out anything?" I wasn't sure if her voice sounded anxious or not.

"I'll be there," I said and hung up.

I lit a cigarette and put my feet up on the desk. The time was now twenty minutes to one o'clock. I was feeling faintly hungry. I was back now in Pasadena City. I missed Hong Kong. I missed the Chinese food. I thought of Sparrow and his eternal sandwiches without enthusiasm, but the body had to be kept alive. After I had planned what to say and do when I got to Jefferson's residence, I locked up the office and went down to Sparrow's snack bar. I kept him fascinated for twenty minutes telling him about the Chinese girls. The hamburger and beer seemed pretty heavy after the Chinese food.

After lunch I went back to my apartment. I shaved, showered and put on a change of clothes. It was then time to drive to J. Wilbur Jefferson's residence.

The butler let me in, still gloomy, still silent. He took me directly to Janet West's office where she was working at her desk.

She looked pale and her eyes were dark-ringed as if she had been sleeping badly. Her smile didn't reach her eyes as she stood up as I came into the room.

"Come in, Mr. Ryan," she said. "Please sit down."

I came on in and sat down. The butler faded away like a replica of Hamlet's ghost.

She sat down, resting her slim hands on the blotter, her eyes troubled, she studied me.

"Did you have a successful trip? Mr. Jefferson will be ready to see you in ten minutes."

"Yes, I had a pretty successful trip," I said. I took from my wallet the photograph of Frank Belling she had given to me and flicked it onto her desk. "You gave me that—remember? You told me it was a photograph of Herman Jefferson."

She looked at the photograph, her face expressionless, then she looked at me. "Yes, I know."

116

"I'm going to show it to Mr. Jefferson and I'm going to tell him you gave it to me, telling me it is a photograph of his son."

She looked down at her hands, then she said, "Is he dead?"

"Herman? Yes, he's dead now."

I saw a shiver run through her and for a long moment she remained motionless, than she looked up. She was pale and there was a lost expression in her eyes.

"What happened?" she asked.

"Did you know he was hooked up in a drug traffic racket?"

"Yes . . . I knew."

"Well, they caught up with him. He tried a double-cross that didn't come off. How did you know?"

She didn't say anything for some seconds.

"Oh, he told me," she said wearily. "You see, I was stupid enough to fall in love with him. He played on that. I've been a hopeless fool about him, but some women do make fools of themselves over worthless men."

"Why did you give me this photograph and tell me it was Herman's?"

"I wanted to shield Mr. Jefferson. He is the only decent, generous person I have ever known. I couldn't bear to let him find out his son was a drug pedlar."

"Where did you get the photograph from?"

"Herman sent it to me. Although he only wrote once a year to his father, he wrote more often to me." She hesitated, then went on. "You may as well know the truth. We had an affair together years ago. I had his child. Although I knew he was utterly worthless I loved him. He knew that and he played on my feelings. He often sent me snapshots of various people he met. Photographs of Chinese girls. He knew he was upsetting me . . . it amused him. Then suddenly he sent this photograph of Belling. He said he and Belling were going into business together. I suppose he sent the photograph to prove he wasn't lying. I don't know, but he sent it. He asked me to lend him a thousand dollars so he could make a fresh start. I didn't send it to him. Then I had a frantic letter from him saying he was in bad trouble. He was terrified. I could tell that by the way he wrote. He said he had got mixed up with a drug organisation and they were going to kill him. He said he was going into hiding. He told me Belling was dead, but these people thought it was he who was dead. He said his wife would bring Belling's body back here. It was the only way to convince these people he was dead and once they were convinced, they would stop hunting for him." She lifted her hands helplessly. "I was shocked to know he had sunk so low. I didn't want Mr. Jefferson to find out. I know I shouldn't have done it . . . but I did."

As I said nothing, she went on, "He gave me the address of a Chinese. His name was Wong Hop Ho. He told me to write to this man if anything went wrong. When his wife was murdered and when Mr. Jefferson said he was sending you to Hong Kong, I wrote to this man Wong and warned him. I told him I had given you Belling's photograph. I was desperately anxious that Mr. Jefferson shouldn't know the truth."

"He's got to know the truth now," I said. "I can't keep it away from him."

"Why can't you?" She leaned forward. "Why can't he die, thinking his son was decent?"

"It's too complicated for that. The coffin has to be examined. The police are in on this now. This is something that can't be hushed up." I studied her. "I'll keep you out of it, but that's the best I can do."

There came a tap on the door and the butler came in.

"Mr. Jefferson is ready to see you now," he said. "Will you come this way?"

I went with him, leaving Janet staring bleakly out of the window.

J. Wilbur Jefferson was reclining on the bed-chair as if he hadn't moved since the last time I had met him. He watched me come towards him and he waved me to a chair near his.

"Well, young man, so you're back. I take it you have information for me."

I sat down.

"Yes . . . but not the kind of information you're going to welcome," I said. "You sent me to Hong Kong to get the background of this thing and I've got it."

He studied me, then shrugged his shoulders.

"Go ahead and tell me. What did you find out?"

I gave him an edited version of what had happened in Hong Kong and what I had found out about his son. I didn't tell him how his son had died. I said the police had found his body in the sea.

He listened, staring across at a row of standard roses, his face expressionless. He said nothing until I had finished.

"And now?" he asked, still not looking at me.

"The police want to open the coffin," I said. "They want your permission to open the vault."

"That's all right. They can get the key from Miss West."

"I have arranged for your son's body to be sent back here," I went on. "It'll arrive at the end of the week."

"Thank you," he said indifferently.

There was a long pause while I looked down at my feet, waiting and he stared bleakly in front of him.

"I never thought Herman would have sunk as low as that," he said finally. "A drug trafficker . . . the lowest animal on earth."

I didn't say anything.

"Well, I suppose he is better off dead," he went on. "Now about his wife . . . you haven't found out who killed her?"

"Not yet. Do you want me to go on trying?"

"Why not?" I could see he was thinking about his son. "If there is anything you want, any money you want, Miss West will attend to it. We may as well make a tidy end to this sordid business. Find who killed her."

"I'll want the key to the vault," I said, and got to my feet. "There is one other thing, Mr. Jefferson. Now your son is dead, who will be your heir?"

That startled him. He gazed at me blankly.

"What business is it of yours who gets my money?"

"Is it that much of a secret? If it is, I apologise."

He frowned, moving his heavily-veined hands uneasily along the arms of his chair.

"No, it's no secret, but why do you ask?"

"If Herman's wife had lived, would she have had a mention in your Will?"

"Of course. My son's wife would have been entitled to have received what I was leaving to him."

"Was it a large amount?"

"Half my money."

"That would be a large amount. Who gets the other half?"

"Miss West."

"So now she'll get the lot?"

He stared thoughtfully at me.

"That is right. Why are you so curious about my personal affairs, Mr. Ryan?"

"It's my business to be curious," I said and I left him.

I found Janet West at her desk. She looked up as I stood in the doorway.

"Come in, Mr. Ryan," she said, her voice cold and flat.

I came in.

"I want the key to the vault," I said. "The police will want to open the coffin. I promised Lieutenant Retnick to get the key for him. Mr. Jefferson doesn't object."

She searched in a drawer of her desk and then gave me a key.

"I told him the story," I said, dropping the key into my pocket. "He took it pretty well."

She lifted her shoulders in a resigned shrug.

"And now?"

"He wants me to find Jo-An's killer. That's my next job."

"How will you do that?"

"Most murders start from a motive," I said. "I'm pretty sure there is a motive for this one. I even have an idea what the motive is. Well, I mustn't take up your time. I'll return the key when I've finished with it."

I left her, staring thoughtfully down at her desk. The butler let me out. He said nothing. I had nothing to say to him. As I walked over to my car I saw a movement behind the curtains of Janet West's window.

She was watching me leave.

2

Lieutenant Retnick and Sergeant Pulski got out of the police car and joined me at the cemetery gates.

"If there's one place I hate visiting," Retnick said around the cigar he was holding in his teeth, "it's a burial field."

"We'll all arrive here sooner or later," I said. "It's your future, permanent home."

"I know. You don't have to tell me," Retnick growled. "I just don't like permanent homes."

We walked through the open gateway and up a broad roadway flanked on either side by expensive-looking tombs.

"It's over there," Pulski said, pointing to an alley to our right. "Fourth one in the row."

We walked down the alley until we came to a massive marble tomb, surrounded with marble chippings and a marble kerb.

"This is it," Pulski said and took the key I handed to him.

"How did old man Jefferson react?" Retnick asked as he watched Pulski approach the door to the tomb. "I bet he had things to say to you, shamus."

"Hey!" There was a startled note in Pulski's voice as he turned to face us. "Someone's been here before us!"

Retnick moved forward. I kept pace with him. We saw Pulski push the vault door open. The lock had been broken. We could see where some kind of lever had been inserted between the door and the lock. The marble was cracked and a piece had been broken off. There had been a lot of hurried pressure exerted to break the lock.

"Don't touch anything," Retnick warned Pulski. "Let's take a look."

He threw the beam of a flashlight into the vault. There were four coffins on shelves facing us. The one on the lowest shelf was without a lid. The lid stood against the wall of the tomb. We moved forward and looked into the coffin. There was a long bar of lead lying on the floor of the coffin, but nothing else.

Retnick said, "Well, for Pete's sake! Looks like someone's snatched the body!"

"Could be there was never a body in it," I said.

He turned on me, his face snarled up with impatient anger.

"What do you mean? Just how much do you know you haven't told me?"

"I've told you all I know," I said curtly. "But that still doesn't stop me using my brains, does it?"

He turned savagely to Pulski.

"Get this box to headquarters and give it the treatment. Could be there are fingerprints on it. Me and this smart shamus are going for a walk." He grabbed hold of my arm and shoved me out of the tomb while Pulski walked down the alley to the police car where he started to talk to headquarters over the car's telephone.

When he was out of hearing, Retnick sat on one of the tombs and fed a cigar into his face.

"Come on, shamus, give. What's on your goddam mind?"

"Right now there's nothing on my mind," I said. "Would it worry you to know you're sitting on someone's dead wife, husband or mother?"

"I don't give a damn who I'm sitting on," Retnick snarled. "The Mayor telephoned me this morning . . . my influential brother-in-law . . . he wants to know when I'm going to solve this case." He chewed his cigar savagely. "How do you like that? Even my own brother-in-law puts pressure on me."

"Tough," I said.

"What makes you think there wasn't a body in the coffin?"

"Just an idea. Belling's body was burned to a cinder. Why snatch it? It couldn't be identified anyway. So why take the risk and the trouble to bust open the vault and lug his remains away? Just because Herman's body wasn't in the coffin, I thought Belling's body had to be. Now I don't think anyone's body was in it. The coffin was sent back here loaded with lead. There was no body in it."

Retnick brooded over this.

"Why then should some joker take a look?" he asked.

"That's right." I suddenly saw why. I thumped my fist into the palm of my hand. "I must be more of a dope than I think I am! Of course! It jells! It's one of those goddam simple things I should have seen right from the start!"

Retnick regarded me sourly.

"What are you raving about?" he snarled.

"The heroin was in the coffin!" I said. "Two thousand ounces of it! It was the perfect hiding-place . . . the perfect means of smuggling it out of Hong Kong to here!"

Retnick stared at me, then he jumped to his feet.

"Yeah . . . that makes sense! Looks like we've got ourselves an idea!"

"After Jefferson hijacked the stuff," I said, "he found he was stuck with it. He couldn't leave Hong Kong and the organisation were hunting for him. That amount of heroin must be worth a pile of money. Jefferson had to convince the organisation he was dead. So he killed two birds with one stone. He got Jo-An to write to his father for money to bring his body home. Remember, he

121

had no money. The only way to get the heroin out was in the coffin with old man Jefferson paying to get it out. Belling's body was put in the coffin and cleared through the American Consul for shipment home. At some stage, the body was removed and probably dumped in the sea. The drugs and the lead weight were put in the coffin. Although Jefferson was trapped in Hong Kong, he did make sure his wife and the heroin were safe."

"Who's knocked the stuff off?" Retnick asked hopefully.

"How should I know? MacCarthy told me when they found Jefferson's body he had been given a working over. Maybe the organisation got the truth out of him and sent a man over here to break open the vault and grab the stuff. I wouldn't know."

Retnick's face brightened.

"Makes sense. Well then, this isn't my goddam pigeon. The Narcotic Squad will have to take care of this headache." He beamed at me. "Don't let anyone persuade you to use your head for a door-stop. You've got brains even if you don't show them."

"Still doesn't explain why the Chinese girl came to my office and got shot," I said.

His smile slipped and he scowled.

"Yeah."

"I'm working on the idea the killing had nothing to do with the heroin," I said. "Jo-An was to have come into half old man Jefferson's money. He told me so this afternoon. I also found out now she's dead, his secretary, Janet West, gets the lot."

Retnick squinted at me.

"You think she killed her?"

"No, I don't, but she's got a ten million dollar motive. I told you before: she could have an ambitious boy friend. But that still doesn't explain how the girl came to be shot in my office."

Retnick scratched his head.

"Maybe I'd better check to see if she has a boy friend," he said reluctantly.

Pulski called to him.

"Keep in touch, shamus," Retnick said. "I've got things to do," and he hurried down the alley towards Pulski who was holding the telephone receiver and beckoning to him.

I drove back to my office block. The time was half past five. I had no idea why I was going back to my office. I certainly had nothing to do, but there seemed no point in my going back to my apartment. I unlocked the door, entered the outer room, unlocked my office door and crossed to the window and opened it. Then I sat down, lit a cigarette and stared at the bust and buttock calendar on the wall facing me.

I thought of Janet West. I thought of the mysterious John Hardwick. Was this man who called himself Hardwick Janet's boy friend? Had he killed Herman Jefferson's wife? If he had then why the hell had he picked on my office to do the job and why had he tried to implicate me in the murder?

Somehow I couldn't imagine Janet West implicated in a murder. She just wasn't the type. And yet there was the ten million dollar motive. Maybe the boy friend had done it and hadn't told her about it . . . maybe . . .

I heard Jay Wayde's voice. It broke into my concentration. He said, "I'll get off now. See you in the morning." His voice came clearly from his open window through mine. I heard him leave and half expected him to look in on me, but he didn't. He walked heavy-footed to the elevator. A moment later I heard the elevator descend.

I went back to my thoughts: they didn't get me anywhere.

I sat there, brooding, trying to get an idea on which to work for over an hour, then suddenly I heard the distant sound of an aircraft engine. It became loud and then faded and I found myself sitting bolt upright in my chair. The noise of a jet-propelled aircraft taking-off followed. I remembered hearing these sounds coming over the telephone when John Hardwick had telephoned me, asking me to go out and watch the deserted bungalow on Connaught Boulevard. I got swiftly to my feet and listened. The sound of a busy airport came through my open window. I had no doubt where it was coming from. I went into the passage, aware my heart was thumping, and moving silently to Jay Wayde's office door, I turned the handle and eased open the door.

Wayde's secretary, the one with the glasses and the mousey look was bending over the tape recorder I had already noticed on Wayde's desk. The band was running through the playback head and from the loudspeaker came the busy sounds of an aircraft landing and taking-off.

"For a moment I thought you had turned into an airport," I said.

She nearly jumped out of her skin. Hastily turning off the recorder, she spun around, her pale washed-out blue eyes wide with shock.

I smiled disarmingly at her.

"I didn't mean to startle you," I said. "I heard the noise and I was curious."

"Oh. . . ." She relaxed a little. "I—I shouldn't be doing this. I—I wondered what was on the tape. Mr. Wayde has gone home."

"Play it again . . . it sounded a good recording."

She hesitated.

"No . . . I—I don't think I'd better. Mr. Wayde might not like it."

"He won't mind." I wandered over to the desk. She gave ground, moving away from me. "Nice machine." I pressed the rewind button. When the tape was ready to play again I pressed down the playback button. The sounds of a busy airport came clearly through the loudspeaker. I stood listening for maybe a couple of minutes, then I switched off the machine and smiled at her.

I was pretty excited for I was sure now I had at last found the mysterious John Hardwick. I had found him by a fantastic stroke of luck and by this scared-looking girl's curiosity.

"Mr. Wayde won't be back until tomorrow?" I asked.

"No."

"Well, okay, I'll see him tomorrow then. Good night," and I went out and into my office where I sat at my desk and lit a cigarette with hands that shook a little from my excitement.

I sat there for half an hour. Then a few minutes after six I heard the girl leave the office, lock up and walk away down the passage. I waited for the whine of the descending elevator as it took her down to the ground floor. I waited until I heard the sounds of the other workers leaving the offices along my corridor. I waited until there was no sound to tell me anyone remained up there. Then I got to my feet and went to my door, opened it and looked out into the passage. No lights showed behind any of the glass-panelled doors. I had the floor now to myself.

I went back to my desk and opening a drawer, took out a bunch of skeleton keys. It took me less than a minute to unlock Jay Wayde's office door. I entered and locked the door after me. I stood looking around. There was a big green steel and fireproof cupboard against one of the walls. I examined the lock. None of my keys would open it. I went back to my office and collected a few tools, returned and once more locked myself in Wayde's office.

I spent fifteen minutes trying to open the cupboard, but the lock beat me. I hesitated, wondering if I should bust open the cupboard, but decided against it. I looked in the other room. It contained a desk, a typewriter, a chair and a filing cabinet. I looked into the filing cabinet but there was nothing in there but papers.

If what I was looking for was in the office at all, it would be locked in the steel cupboard.

I took the airport recording off the tape recorder and put another tape I found in the desk drawers onto the machine. I turned off the lights and leaving the door wide open I went into my office.

I locked the tape away, then I turned up Wayde's home address in the telephone book. His apartment was on Laurence Avenue, a ten-minute drive from his office. I called the number, but there was no answer.

I wondered if I should call Retnick, but I wanted to sew up this case on my own. I could still be wrong, but I didn't think so. I decided there was time to call Retnick after I had talked to Wayde.

I kept calling Wayde's number. Finally, a little after nine o'clock, he answered.

"This is Nelson Ryan," I said.

"Why, hello!" He sounded surprised. "Anything I can do for you? Did you have a good trip?"

"Fine . . . I'm in my office. I looked in to pick up something I'd forgotten. I found your office door wide open and the lights off. Your girl's gone. Looks like she's forgotten to lock up. Do you want me to get the janitor to lock up for you?"

I heard him catch his breath sharply.

"That's damned odd," he said after a long pause. "Maybe I'd better come down."

"Doesn't look as if you have had a burglar."

"There's nothing to steal in there except my recorder and the typewriter. I guess I'd better come down all the same."

"Suit yourself. I can get the janitor to lock up if you like."

"No, it's all right. I'd rather come down. I can't understand her forgetting to lock up. She's never done that before."

"Maybe she's in love," I laughed. "Well, I'm leaving now. Sure you don't want me to do anything?"

"No, thanks, and thanks for calling."

"Think nothing of it . . . so long."

I hung up and turned off the lights. I locked up my office and then went into Wayde's office. I went into his secretary's room and sat on the desk. I took out my gun and clicked back the safety-catch. I put the gun on the desk beside me.

I had about ten minutes to wait before I heard the whine of the ascending elevator. I got off the desk and stood behind the door, gun in hand. I heard quick footfalls then movements in Wayde's office. The light turned on, the door closed. I peered through the door crack. Wayde stood looking around. He walked to the room in which I was, pushed the door back against me and looked in, then he stepped back into his office. I heard a jangle of keys, then a lock snap back. I guessed he had opened the steel cupboard.

I stepped out from behind the door. He was kneeling in front of the cupboard. The double doors of the cupboard stood wide open. The cupboard was packed with bottles, boxes, glass files and other chemist's samples.

"Is the heroin still there?" I asked quietly.

He gave a shudder, then looked slowly over his shoulder to stare at me. I lifted the gun slightly so he could see it. His face went chalk-white and slowly he rose to his feet.

"What are you doing here?" he asked, his voice husky.

"I tried to open the cupboard but the lock beat me," I said, watching him. "So I thought it was an idea if you came down and opened it for me. Move away and don't start anything."

"Why should I?" he said and walked unsteadily to his desk

125

and slumped down into his chair. He buried his face in his hands. I glanced into the bottom of the cupboard. There were about fifty small, neatly packed parcels lying on the floor of the cupboard.

"Those the drugs Jefferson hijacked?" I asked, coming over to the desk and sitting on the edge of it.

He leaned back, rubbing his white, sweating face.

"Yes. How did you know I had them?"

"You forgot to take the tape recording of the airport off the machine. Your girl played it back. I heard it. The whole set-up fell into place," I told him.

"I've always been forgetful. If there's a mistake to be made, I make it. I knew when you said you were going to Hong Kong I was sunk." He looked wearily at me. "I knew somewhere along the line you'd come across a loose thread that would lead you to me. When you told me you were going, I was insane enough to hire a junkie to kill you. That's how desperate I was! When that didn't work, I knew it was only a matter of time, but I was so hopelessly involved there was nothing else I could do but hang on and hope."

"If it's any satisfaction to you, you nearly got away with it," I said, "I thought Jefferson's secretary was the one. She had the motive and I'm a sucker for motives."

"I hoped you would pick on her," he said. "That's why I told you about her affair with Herman, but I knew if you ran into him in Hong Kong and you talked to him you were certain to get onto me."

"How did you know Jo-An was coming back here with the heroin?"

"It was all arranged. That stuff I told you about Herman was true, but I lied when I told you I didn't like him. We had always been friends. We always kept in touch. For the past two years now I've been struggling to keep this business of mine going. I just haven't the knack for business. I haven't the knack for anything come to that. I guess that's why Herman and I were friends. He hadn't the knack for anything either. Things got so bad here, I was desperate for money. Then Herman wrote me. He said he had got his hands on a large consignment of heroin and would I buy it off him? As an industrial chemist I have a number of safe outlets for handling heroin, but of course, I hadn't the money. He was stupid enough to tell me he was trapped in Hong Kong and unless Jo-An could raise the money to get him a false passport and his fare home, he would be dead in a few weeks. He said the organisation he had double-crossed were hunting for him, and if they found him, they would kill him. I saw my chance of at last laying my hands on a big sum of money. If I could get the heroin, I could sell it at a very high profit. So I wrote to him and told him I'd buy the stuff. It was arranged that Jo-An

126

should come straight to me from the airport and hand over the stuff and get the money, but Herman didn't tell me on what plane she was coming. I didn't dare ask in case the query was traced back to me. I knew I would have to kill her." He stared down at his big, shaking hands. "At the time, it didn't seem so bad planning to kill a Chinese girl, but I couldn't think how I was to get rid of her body. It was then I finally decided to plant her body in your office. You were next door to me so it would be easy. You were a private investigator. She might be taken for a client of yours. I thought when the police investigated the murder, with you involved, the trail would get so confused, they wouldn't think of me. I had to be sure you would be out of your office when she arrived. I had this airport recording I'd taken when I first bought the recorder. I was scared to go to the airport in case I was spotted so I used the recorder to convince you I was calling from the airport, giving me a reasonable excuse why I didn't come to see you. When you had gone, I waited and waited. I thought she would never come. Finally, she arrived. She trusted me. She told me the heroin was in the coffin. I very nearly didn't kill her." He closed his eyes for a moment. "She was such a pretty little thing. I had got into your office and taken your gun. While she talked, I took the gun from the desk drawer, keeping it out of sight. Then she asked me for the money. That decided me. I lifted the gun and shot her." He shuddered and again wiped his sweating face. "I carried her into your office . . . I left her there. Well, it's a relief it's over. I haven't been able to sleep. I couldn't even sell the stuff. It's all there. I've been waiting and waiting and waiting for you to come back. When I knew you were back, I just hadn't the nerve to face you." He looked imploringly at me. "What are you going to do?"

I had no pity for him. He had tried to involve me in murder. He had hired a thug to kill me. He had brutally shot Herman's wife, but to me what was unforgivable, he had been responsible without knowing it for Leila's death. He had plotted and planned with cold, ferocious greed and he had betrayed a friend even though the friend had been as worthless as himself.

"What do you think?" I said. "You'll have to tell your sordid tale to the police."

I picked up the telephone receiver. As I began to dial, he slid out of his chair and started to walk unsteadily towards the door. I suppose I could have stopped him by shooting him in the leg, but I couldn't be bothered. He wouldn't get far. My job was to stay here and make sure the heroin remained where it was until Retnick arrived.

As I was telling the desk sergeant at police headquarters to alert Retnick and get a squad car down to me fast, I heard Wayde take the elevator to the ground floor. The squad car only just missed him, but they picked him up half an hour later. They found him in his car at the far end of Beach Drive. He had taken a cyanide capsule: one of the advantages of being an industrial chemist. He had taken the quick, easy way out.

Retnick listened to my story, a sour expression on his face.

"I was well off the beam," I concluded. "I would have bet a dollar Jefferson's secretary was the one. It was by the purest chance I got onto Wayde. If he hadn't made the mistake of keeping the airport recording on his machine and if his girl hadn't been curious, I don't think I would have got onto him."

Retnick offered me a cigar.

"Look, Ryan," he said. "I've got to have the credit for cracking this case. I've got a reputation to look after: you haven't. If you want my co-operation in the future, you'll keep in the shade. I'll handle all the publicity."

"You remember me . . . I'll remember you," I said. "We must think up some music to go with that one, but watch your step, Lieutenant. Old man Jefferson will want this kept quiet. He won't let it be known his son was a drug pedlar if he can help it. If you want him to remember you in a nice way, you'll go awfully slow on any publicity. You're lucky Wayde is dead."

I left him staring moodily down at the floor. The only person of the whole sorry lot I felt sorry about was the little Chinese, Leila.

I was still thinking about her as I walked across to Sparrow's quick snack bar for another lonely supper.